Kooshma's Dabria

Dytania Johnson

authorHOUSE®

AuthorHouse™
1663 Liberty Drive
Bloomington, IN 47403
www.authorhouse.com
Phone: 833-262-8899

Published by AuthorHouse 07/26/2024

ISBN: 979-8-8230-1610-0 (sc)
ISBN: 979-8-8230-1609-4 (e)

Print information available on the last page.

This book is printed on acid-free paper.

Contents

INTRODUCTION TO THE BACKSTORY

Understanding signifying this unchangeable aspect in the Kooshma trilogy relies on comprehending the events that transpired in the past. Let me explain.

People with African heritage and those with darker skin tones, who did not have a Caucasian background, exuded this quality by using manipulation tactics and fabricating false accusations. The slave master's wife coerced Kooshma, a slave, into engaging in sexual activities with her. One fateful day, the bell signaled the daring escape of the enslaved, shattering the long-standing era of secrecy surrounding their illicit affair.

Upon entering his home, Mr. Wilcox was confronted by an unexpected scene - his wife and Kooshma during a sexual act. True to form, Mrs. Wilcox wasted no time in screaming that she had been the victim of rape. Swiftly, Kooshma dashed from the room towards the swamp. The insects swarmed onto Kooshma's bare flesh, taking advantage of his vulnerable state. Though unbearable, the conditions were not as bad as the fate awaiting him if recaptured. Their relentless pursuit of Kooshma ended when they apprehended him. Mrs. Wilcox created a damning account of rape, making Kooshma the ultimate warning for other slaves to comply. The overseers beat and raped Kooshma's wife and kids as Kooshma watched. He pleaded for forgiveness to spare his wife and daughters because his life being taken was more justified. It reminded all slaves that disobedience would not be tolerated.

Master Wilcox, who once thought Kooshma was a trustworthy slave, subjected him to days without food in a dark cellar. To Kooshma's horror, he discovered they had given him food made from the dismembered remains of his own family. Driven by revenge, he made a dark pact with a vengeful voodoo witch, offering his soul for the torment and demise of the overseers and master Wilcox, leaving them begging for death and condemned to eternal damnation.

Generations came and departed, yet Kooshma's relentless pursuit of Master Wilcox's bloodline endured, resulting in countless casualties. Inflicting even crueler deaths for each person who dared to rest. Unfortunately, those that was not of African descent weren't exempt, being that Master Wilcox and the overseers had sexual relations with any slave of their choosing. Which resulted in their bloodline being infused with African Americans by default. The dying of the Wilcox's pure bloodline left unclaimed properties led to the coming together a reunion of sorts for staking a claim to the Wilcox plantation.

The decision to renovate the property set in motion a series of events that led to the dramatic revival of Kooshma, uncovering hidden family secrets, deceit, and tragedy. Get ready for the gripping conclusion of the trilogy as we enter KOOSHMA'S DABRIA.

PROLOGUE

The child, born from a dormant evil, endured trauma in her life, confronted ostracism from her peers, and received rejection from past adopters. Strange things unexplained have found a permanent home catching the eyes of childless parents, Mr. and Mrs. Mason. Shantell's behavior, brushed aside as mere outbursts, will no longer plague Miss Flackman's adoption agency. Her sudden attack on a child with scissors revealed her malicious nature that cannot be controlled. Packed up and eager to leave the grounds of the adoption agency, Shantell rushed towards the car with her small bag of clothing in hand. Wondering if that was all Shantell had, Mrs. Mason asked, and Shantell responded, in a shameless manner.

"Yes ma'am."

She has never had much. For her, a small bag held everything she needed. The bag possibly contained just a couple of clothing changes. Worn-out shoes and a toe hole indicate the need for shopping. Thank you, Mr. and Mrs. Mason, on behalf of myself and the staff for caring for Shantell.

"Thank you, we will let you know how Shantell adjusts."

Veronica expressed her hopes that Shantell's transition would be easier, having already been with families of a different race.

"No worries. Shantell, regardless of color, does not engage in perceiving white or black as an issue. She just needs love and patience."

"Understanding the fact that it may require some time for a ten-year-old to adjust, my husband and I will persist in showing her what other adoptive parents haven't, apart from the homes you mentioned."

Miss Flackman extended her hand, wearing a warm smile. "I appreciate hearing that. "Goodbye Shantell."

With a wave, Shantell took her leave from Miss Flackman.

"Bye," said Miss Flackman.

Waving while she watched the car drive away into the distance. Making her way towards one of the staff members, Mrs. Collins, Miss Flackman, walked towards her from the side of the building, exiting the playground.

"Miss Flackman, I didn't want to bring this up in front of the Masons, but when I was getting some of Shantell's paperwork together, the counselor's and psychiatrist's files were missing."

Miss Flackman glanced at Mrs. Collins with a side eye, hinting for a mutual understanding.

"Everyone knows the reason I took them away from you and everyone else here. Let's hope Shantell never returns. Her actions and words defy normalcy and challenge my beliefs. We should have dealt with her long ago. Should she ever return, God forbid, I will ensure that no one ever must sacrifice their lives for her, even if it means sacrificing mine."

They both walked through the playground, stopped and stared at the tree that Shantell etched the name Dabria into. Mrs. Collins looked at Miss Flackman.

"Who do you think Dabria is?"

"I'm unsure, Mrs. Collins, but please make sure you take care of it and remove it within the hour. I hope that the other kids forget about Shantell, by erasing any evidence of her existence."

CHAPTER1

Home Sweet Home

Moments before her return home to the small town of Old Say brook, Connecticut, Veronica turned around and started a casual conversation to ease the awkward silence.

"If you'd like, Shantell, we could play a game." Shantell responded with a burst of enthusiasm.

"What kind of game?"

Veronica clarified, "It's just a fun activity to help us become more familiar with each other."

Tom smiled at his wife and chimed in, "I agree, honey."

"What a brilliant suggestion! I'll start it off," said

Veronica. "Ummu, I like strawberry ice cream." Veronica started, prompting the next person to share. A sense of sadness was clear on Shantell's face.

"What's wrong Shantell?" asked Veronica.

"I don't know any other kinds of ice cream," said Shantell. "Just vanilla, we weren't allowed to have any other flavors at the orphanage."

Veronica hid her pain behind a composed facade, concealing her genuine emotions. Shantell's voice trembled, and she struggled to hold back tears, expressing her profound sadness.

"Well, you know what"? asked Veronica. "Right after we fill the car with gas and a quick oil check, we will get you some ice cream of any flavor you want."

"Can we go now?" asked Shantell.

Just a little longer," replied Veronica, responding to Shantell's question. Patience is a virtue.

"No, no, no! I want it now.

In a tantrum, Shantell burst out while kicking and screaming. Her tantrum escalated to where she started inflicting scratches on her face and arms. Veronica called out to her husband while he was pumping gas.

"Tom!" screamed Veronica.

In a panic, Veronica attempted to restrain Shantell to prevent further self-inflicted damage. Without hesitation, Tom relinquished his grip on the gas handle, stumbling and falling over the gas hose.

"What did you do? asked Tom.

"What did I do? What do you mean? Why would I hurt her?"

"You know what I mean, I'm just asking."

"I understand your point, but is it necessary to revisit a matter from such a long time ago? Could you tell me why we are still talking about this?" exclaimed Veronica, her exasperation apparent.

"Veronica, I apologize, I just panicked." "Shantell, calm down, pay attention to me!"

Shouted Tom, as he slowly gained control of the situation. Shantell stared into the eyes of Veronica while she spoke to Tom.

"I'm sorry daddy, I didn't mean to be bad. Please don't take me back."

Veronica and Tom looked at each other, stuck on the words mommy and daddy canceled out everything else. They refused to give up because they longed to be parents and were given a second chance.

"You know what?" asked Tom. Let's go get ice cream now."

Shantell's face lit up with joy. They entered the ice cream shop where they were greeted by the shop employee.

"Hello, welcome to Chaney's, the best ice cream that will ever cross your taste buds."

Was a formal introduction given by the ice cream tech. The shop's rehearsed slogan was told to every customer who entered the shop.

"How are you doing today?" asked the ice cream worker.

"Oh my, how do we choose? What do you recommend?"

"Well, most of the adults that come in here seem to enjoy traditional flavors like vanilla, chocolate, and strawberry, also our root beer floats. As for this young lady, my recommendation is our triple decker explosion. A scoop of ice cream with chocolate chip, raspberry, and banana flavors. Tom observed the worker's expression and concluded.

"She will have the triple decker." "Let's sit over there! Tom suggested. That table seems perfect.

Right after settling down, Shantell dug in, only to encounter her first brain freeze. Overwhelmed by pain, she screamed and held onto her head. They found humor in the situation, chuckling.

"Shantell, slow down, that's what happens when you eat or drink something cold too fast. In order to appreciate the flavors of ice cream as a treat you have to take your time, but not to slow or it will melt. That feeling you had in your head is called a brain freeze. Shantell grabbed her head again.

"It sure hurt, but it was worth it."

They shared their first laugh as a family, a pure moment of joy. With a satisfied expression, Shantell held her stomach after finishing the last bite.

"All done, said Shantell."

"Wow," said Tom, "I think that was a record-breaking time. Well, ladies, I think it's time to hit the road."

Shantell's heavy eyelids succumbed to fatigue, despite the countless hours that had gone by. The non-stop excitement frazzled her. Exhausted from the day's events, Veronica turned her attention to Tom.

"She is sound asleep. After almost six months, we have Shantell as an addition to the family. However, we cannot overlook the episode at the gas station," said Tom.

"Which part? asked Veronica. Shantell's outburst? Or the accusation that I was the one that caused it?"

"Veronica, everything happened quickly. I was just as surprised as you!"

"How does your nervousness connect to insinuating my involvement with trying to hurt her?"

"Why discuss this now?" asked Tom.

"Fine, let's just forget it. I understand your intention, but how much longer will you resent me? You said that I should move on, but you won't let me."

The air between them was thick with unresolved emotions as they made their way back home. Tom broke the silence by reaching out to hold her hand, assuring her that things would improve. The car stopped in a peaceful suburban community, where the Mason family resided for six years. Despite their close-knit relationships, this tranquil community experienced occasional disruptions.

"Wake up Veronica, we're home."

She rubbed her eyes to clear the sleepiness that impaired her vision, stretching and yawning.

"Shantell is still fast asleep."

"You unlock the door. After I put Shantell to bed,

perhaps you and I can get some sleep. I'll get the rest of our things from the car in the morning," said Tom.

Veronica opened the door, allowing Tom to carry Shantell out of the car. With her head tucked into the curve of his neck, he strained to hear her soft mutterings,

"Hapana usifanye', 'Hapana usifanye', translation [No don't do it, No don't do it]

He hoped to grasp her words' potential significance for a future discussion. No matter how much he strained to listen, the words remained incomprehensible to him. The words seemed like nonsensical mutterings from a child's fantasy. Tom set Shantell down on her bed. He stood upright and stared at her for a few seconds. He heard a sound, a muffled sob, reminiscent of a young boy trying to suppress his emotions. Overwhelmed, a single tear trickled down his cheek. The sound evoked memories of someone that was significant in his life. Someone from his past, who holds a special place in his heart, occupied his thoughts.

CHAPTER 2

Family Business

The clock ticked away with just a mere three hours remaining until sunrise. The sun rose and soon after, someone arrived, announcing themselves with a doorbell sound. As he descended the stairs, Tom swung open the door and discovered his sister Blair waiting on the other side.

"What are you doing here? "Blair, don't start, okay? It was a long night."

"Tom how are you still married to her after what she did?" asked Blair. "Just make sure you monitor her and please make sure she takes her meds."

Positioned on the stairs, Veronica wore a pained

expression of guilt and regret, aware of her actions but powerless to change them. Ensuring that she remained unnoticed, she retreated to her room and settled in, finding solace in tears as she drifted off to sleep

"Blair, keep your voice down before she hears you.

"Fine Tom, I will leave it alone for now.

"Just come back some other time, Blair, and please remember to call before coming next time.

"Sure, no problem! Make sure you visit your mother soon. She's been asking about you since you last saw her. No one knows the length of our time here. According to Exodus 20:12, to have long days in the land that the Lord gives you, remember to honor your father and mother."

In a composed manner, Tom expressed his understanding of biblical teachings, warning against the selective use of pious quotes.

"Let's not forget that pole you used to dance on before your so-called found religion. As you judge my wife, do not forget your own flaws. I think it's time for you to go. In fact, cancel that visit until you can learn to respect my wife and he slammed the door in Blair's face.

Upon making his way back to bed, Tom was awakened by the joyful sounds of singing and the amazing aroma of Shantell's first home-cooked meal filling the air in her new home. Shantell hopped out of bed and into her slippers. The savory sweet smell of blueberry pancakes and sausage were all she wanted to get to, so she rushed towards the kitchen. With precision, Veronica poured orange juice into glasses while standing at the counter in a daze.

"What's wrong mommy?" asked Shantell?"

In order not to alarm Shantell, Veronica wiped her tears dry before turning around.

"Oh, nothing honey, just preparing breakfast and thinking about how happy we are to finally have you here as Our Daughter."

Veronica pressed her palm on Shantell's cheek. I cooked a little bit of everything, not knowing what you would like. I hope you enjoy it. By filling Shantell's plate, Veronica provided her with five slices of bacon, three sausages, and five pancakes. Shantell looked over at her, confused.

"Mommy, stop! That's too much.

Continuing, Veronica seemed as though she didn't hear Shantell. Piling on even more food, adding eggs and waffles. Shantell shouts!

"Mommy that's enough!"

Food flew from the table onto the floor. After hiding behind a facade for some time, the entity finally started to emerge.

CHAPTER 3

Evil can't be contained

Noticing the sound of dishes breaking and chaos downstairs, Tom hurried towards the kitchen to find Veronica as Shantell fell to the floor.

"What happened?"

Confused, Veronica tried to communicate as best as she could.

"I'm still trying to make sense of it all. In an instant, I went from making breakfast to being on the floor with you watching me."

Slowly gaining consciousness, Shantell woke up to the sounds of someone desperately trying to wake her.

"Daddy? Whispered Shantell. What happened?"

Tom reassured her that everything was ok. He picked her up gently.

"It's ok honey daddy's here."

Tom glanced at his wife and suggested she see Dr. Whittman again.

"Did you remember to take your prescribed medication Veronica?" asked Tom.

Ignoring the question, Veronica avoided eye contact and started clearing the floor of food and debris. The unaddressed inquiry offered Tom the information he was seeking. Frustrated by the unresolved inquiry, he sighed and escorted Shantell to her room.

"Shantell, we'll give you some time to rest, and if you're feeling better, we can all go shopping together as a family and get you a fresh wardrobe."

"Clothes, asked Shantell? New clothes for me?"

"Absolutely, we must ensure you're all set to begin classes. Are you excited?"

"I guess so, but I'm also sort of scared."

"It's normal to feel scared, but I promise everything will be okay. Your kindness will attract friends, I'm sure of it."

"I hope so. It was different when I was in the orphanage and other homes."

"No worries, baby girl, get some rest."

As Veronica tries to enter the room, Tom exits and stops her.

"I don't think you should bother her right now because she needs to rest," said Tom. Also, Veronica, it doesn't concern me whether you like it. I'm going to call Dr. Whittman and make an appointment. It's been over a year since you've seen her. I thought the meds would be enough. Since you haven't been taking then I can't go through this again. Especially now that we have Shantell, there's only so long we can keep this from her. She needs stability."

"Okay, I'll go," Veronica said.

Tom let out a sigh of relief, feeling overjoyed that she didn't put up a fight.

CHAPTER 4

The first day of school

A loud alarm awakens Shantell at 6 am, echoing in the house. Unbeknownst to her, she had slept through the entire previous day and night. The level of excitement was beyond her expectations. Filled with anticipation, she jumped out of bed, readying herself for the long-awaited day that would lead to extraordinary achievements.

"Whoa honey, don't you want to eat breakfast?" Veronica asked.

"No, mommy, I'm too excited!"

Veronica, hoping to move on from yesterday's

strange breakfast mishap, started a conversation to kick-start the morning.

"You appear enthusiastic about starting school, that's great. Glad you're getting to know more kids from the neighborhood."

"Yes, I am. Kids in other orphanages and homes didn't treat me well. My white hair made everyone think I was weird. Both children and adults reminded me that I wasn't wanted, but we showed them, didn't we, mommy?

"Yes, honey, we did. Overjoyed with a sense of completion, a mother was the only thing she wanted to be."

"Tom, hurry," shouted Veronica. Shantell's about to burst down here, she's ready to go."

"Yea, hurry," yelled Shantell.

"I'm coming, give me 10 minutes.

"Mom, do guys always take forever to get ready?

Umm, well, everyone is different, but yes, your father is slow and that's with me laying his clothes out for work. I can hear him coming downstairs now. Shantell hopped up from her kitchen chair with the remainder of milk above her lip. Tom grabbed Shantell.

"Wait a minute honey.

He took out a handkerchief and wiped away the excess milk from her face.

"Now you're ready!

Veronica walked them to the door. After turning around, Tom leaned in and kissed his wife on the lips.

"Listen Veronica, I love you, always have and remember I will make that appointment for you today."

Shantell cringed while she watched the embrace of her parents.

"Oh my gosh, that's disgusting you guys."

With a chuckle, he walked towards the car, glancing back at Veronica.

"We have ourselves a handful," said Tom.

Veronica responded. "And I wouldn't have it any other way."

"Tom, are you sure you can handle shopping with her? It should be me. I could miss out on a pivotal bonding experience with her."

"I'll make a deal with you. Today, I'll buy an outfit for Shantell so she can attend school. After school ends, you can accompany her to buy the remaining clothes.

"Great idea that's perfect," said Veronica. Have a great day at school," she shouted.

Shantell waved bye while entering the back seat to strap herself in. A ten-minute drive from the clothing store to the school goes by like seconds. Shantell's dreams become reality-based; the butterflies in her stomach made her question whether she was ready for this. Her twitching finger that Tom recognized in his rearview suggested to him that she was a little nervous.

"It's going to be fine," said Tom. Most of the teachers at the school live in our neighborhood and they are very nice. I'll go with you inside to get you registered and perhaps they will let me walk with you to class."

She grabbed her backpack and exited the car but

grabbed Tom's hand before entering the school. Making her way past a few students and staff, her anxiety heightened, sensing that everyone could concentrate on her in a negative manner. Upon entering the principal's office, Shantell's grip got even tighter to Tom's hand.

"Hello, may I help you?" asked the secretary.

"Yes, you sure can." Conveying his purpose. "I'm here to register my daughter for school."

"Your daughter?" The secretary exclaimed.

"Is there something wrong? It's not anyone's business, but yes, we adopted her."

Tom leaned towards the secretary to ensure Shantell didn't hear and whispered to her,

"I don't like your demeanor. You act like this is the first time you have seen an interracial family. Now can you please register my daughter?"

Tom said in a stern voice. The secretary, startled by Tom's sudden confrontation, replied,

"Yes, sir," with a trembling voice.

Shantell stood in front of the glass door, watching as students passed. Memories of her orphanage days came flooding back, where she could recall being scrutinized, hoping that it wouldn't be too reminiscent of her past experiences. Tom handed the secretary the form, and the secretary looked over the registration.

"Ok Mr. Mason, everything looks in order. The school's counselor will be out with Shantell's schedule. She will point you in the right direction to give you guys the quick tour and introduction to her teachers."

"Thank you," said Tom.

The office underwent a noticeable change as soon as the counselor arrived.

"Hello, sorry I don't mean to stare. You must excuse me. Your daughter reminded me of one of my past students. Her white hair is so pretty. Sorry, let me introduce myself. I'm the school counselor, Miss. Sanchez, but all the parents call me Francine. What do you think about our school so far, Shantell?"

"I don't know anyone here."

"I promise you will make friends. In fact, my daughter is in the class we're going to now, her name is Melanie.

Mrs. Clemens welcomed the gossip group for the class introduction. The children lowered their voices just enough so that Mrs. Clemens didn't get too irate. Despite being very nice, she's reputed for being quite stern. And no one cared to push her to that point.

"Come closer Shantell," said Mrs. Clemens. "Stand beside me and tell everyone a little about yourself."

All eyes were on Shantell. Snickering from a few kids made Shantell feel uncomfortable.

"Alright kids, I want quiet," shouted Mrs. Clemens. "Shantell, would you like to tell the class a little about yourself?"

Shantell gazed, shaking her head in silence.

"Maybe later, when she becomes more comfortable with everyone. Ok Shantell, just have a seat there in the front," said Mrs. Clemens.

Shantell walked towards her assigned desk and took a seat.

"Mrs. Clemens, may I talk to you in the hall," asked Miss. Sanchez.

"Sure."

"Ok class. She cleared her throat and took a sip of water. Excuse me Miss. Sanchez, my throat gets dry. I'll be back to class, carry on where we left off in your English books."

Mrs. Clemens and Miss Sanchez engaged in a conversation in the hallway, clear from the expressions on their faces. The discomforting encounter escalated when both Miss. Sanchez and Mrs. Clemens locked eyes with Shantell.

"Miss. Sanchez, I would love to explain a few things regarding Shantell. She is a unique student that may need special attention. I looked at her file and she moved around a lot from one orphanage to the next since birth. Ostracized all her life, this may be the opportunity she needs to have a solid foundation. I'm hoping she will get along with the kids and make friends with no complications. So, if you can please monitor her progress and report to me anything that may seem to be a concern, I would appreciate it."

Mrs. Clemens put her head down and shook it side to side with empathy for Shantell's past situations. Snickering spreads in class, from a few to over half of twenty students. The naughty children, led by the funny student, filled their empty pen holders with small paper balls soaked in saliva, resulting in Shantell's untidy hair. Most children were followers to avoid drawing attention to themselves.

Despite the continuous taunting, Shantell sat there unbothered, having grown accustomed to it and almost numb. Instead of dwelling on their behavior, she directed her focus towards those who found joy in hurting others. A harrowing smirk on her face when she turned around to the defiant behavior of them silenced the class in its entirety. The looks on their faces created a baffling look on Mrs. Clemens' face when she re-entered the classroom.

"What's going on?" asked Mrs. Clemens.

Spotting the pieces of saliva-soaked paper dangling from Shantell's hair, she ran towards Shantell.

"OH my god, Shantell, are you ok? Who is to blame for this?"

The class remained silent, as did Shantell. Despite being picked on by multiple students, she sat there, smiling, which seemed unlikely.

"Shantell, will you tell me what happened here? I promise no one else will do anything to you."

'It's ok Mrs. Clemens, I'm ok."

One of the little girls that sat next to her raised her hand.

"Mrs. Clemens."

"Yes Melanie?"

Secretly Shantell signaled to Melanie to avoid mentioning anything. Unbeknownst to Mrs. Clemens, she focused her attention on the hopes that Melanie's hesitant response would prove useful. Mrs. Clemens expressed frustration at the prospect of never discovering the person responsible. At least not today.

"Let it serve as a reminder for those with occasional memory lapses. I don't tolerate bullying. Shantell, join me so we can clean you up in the restroom.

"No!" said Shantell.

With persistence in her voice.

"I mean, I'd rather Melanie come with me, it's just that I feel more comfortable with her. She has been nice to me since I arrived, and she can also show me where the restroom is."

"Very well, said Mrs. Clemens.

Sighing with reluctance. She hesitated, which seemed to last forever. Mrs. Clemens thought about the conversation she had with Miss Sanchez only moments ago.

"Take the pass and return immediately," said Mrs. Clemens.

Filled with eagerness, Josh was the first to raise his hand for a quick errand. He also played the role of being the main instigator among a well-known group of mischief-makers, which led Mrs. Clemens to enforce a rule that required members of that circle to be accompanied by a faculty member when walking the halls. Regrettably, the parents didn't react well to singling out a particular group of kids. She pulled out the second hall pass and handed it to Josh with a firm grip, making it difficult to pull before releasing it into his grasp.

"Come back when you're done, don't have me come looking for you. Do you understand Josh?

"Yes, Mrs. Clemens."

Telling her with the sincerity she wanted to hear. The moment she turned away, he couldn't resist unleashing his inner class clown and stuck his tongue out at her while leaving the classroom, eliciting one last round of laughter from his classmates. Josh caught up with the girls.

"Hey, you two, wait, wait for me."

Melanie turned around.

"Josh, leave us alone. I'm so used to you being funny for the class, but Shantell doesn't deserve to be the butt of your jokes." Josh giggled.

"Butt!

"Keep it down!" Melanie chuckled. Attempting to contain her amusement. "You're going to get us in trouble."

"Whatever! said Josh. So, Shantell, what's with the granny's white hair?

"I was born this way," said Shantell. "Some people don't have a choice on how they look, unlike you having a choice to fix your bad breath."

They could not hold back their peals of laughter.

"That was a good one," said Shantell.

Pointing and laughing towards Josh, made the joke even funnier.

"She got you," said Melanie.

Josh's facial expression showed that his humiliation was fueling his anger as Melanie's words continued to sting. The growing intensity of his emotions drove him to react towards Shantell. A chilling thud resonated through the hallway as she collided with the frigid concrete. Shantell's hand moved towards her hip as Melanie came to her rescue, pulling her back up.

"Josh, that wasn't very nice." said Melanie!

Shantell stood firm and smirked. She stared into Josh's face; it seemed as if time stood still. Her eyes were a captivating sight. The stark contrast between the blackness of her pupils and the whiteness of her eyes served as the backdrop for Dabria's seductive invitation to take control of Shantell's mind. The bleeding from Josh's nose began with a lone drop.

"Eww, Josh your nose is bleeding," said Melanie.

"What?" asked Josh.

The blood flow intensified in response to Josh's inquiry. The blood kept gushing, creating a crimson path that trailed behind Shantell as Josh sprinted down the hallway towards the nurse's office, covering his nose.

"We need to return to class," Melanie said.

"Have you girls seen Josh on the way back to class? Mrs. Clemens asked the girls.

"No! He wasn't anywhere in the halls when we passed.

The classroom intercom interrupted the silence, instructing Mrs. Clemens to make her way to

"I'll come as soon as I can.

Upon being called into the medical office, she appeared bewildered, like anyone in that situation.

Everyone in the class chimed in together. "Yes," Mrs. Clemens.

The moment Mrs. Clemens exited the classroom, Melanie cast a glance at Shantell with unease.

"Why did you lie?" asked Melanie.

"Because all they will do is blame us for what happened."

"But we didn't do anything," said Melanie.

"I know, but Josh may say we did. Just let me do the talking if they ask us questions."

Melanie appeared apprehensive as she sat silently, her face reflecting worry.

"Whose Dabria?" asked Melanie.

"What?" ask Shantell.

"In the hall, all you repeated was "Dabria".

"I don't know," Shantell responded.

With every new occurrence, Shantell's genuine essence seemed to fade. The sound of clanking school bells echoed through the hallways, marking the end of the school day. Kids stormed through the hallways, bumping and squeezing, eager to reach the exit door and kick-start their time of fun and games. After a day of boredom and being confined to an assigned area, Shantell ran into her mother's arms with a firm hug and, from the corner of her eyes, focusing on Josh and his parents. Josh appeared to be on the brink of expressing his fear towards Shantell, but he stayed quiet, concealing his concerns.

"So, honey, how was school?" Veronica asked,

"Slightly dull, but I gained a friend.

"That's wonderful honey. Perhaps your father and I can meet her. What's her name?

"Her name is Melanie, and her mom works here."

"Wow, maybe you can get some brownie points.

No, darling, just kidding. You're an amazing girl. You will do just fine."

On the drive home, Veronica couldn't help but steal occasional glances at Shantell, pondering the thoughts swirling through her daughter's mind, all the while contemplating her own sanity and reflecting on the events of that morning.

"Listen, honey, I have one stop to make to the doctor's office."

"What's wrong mommy? Are you sick?"

"Oh, no, it's just a routine checkup."

Unbeknownst to her, Tom had arranged for Veronica to meet with the psychiatrist out of concern for her worsening depression. Sitting in her car, Veronica gathered her thoughts and took a moment to compose herself before entering the doctor's office.

"Do you have any homework?"

"No, nothing today.

"Ok Shantell, just bring something to keep you occupied.

Hand in hand, Veronica guided Shantell across the street, prioritizing their safety. Veronica couldn't help but reminisce about the emotional journey they had gone through before, when they lost their child, making this moment even more poignant. Overwhelmed by the tragedy of losing their child, Veronica reached a breaking point where she could no longer cope. Through a combination of consistent medication and therapeutic sessions, she gained control over her mental health.

The blaring of car horns shattered the silence,

signaling the urgency to evacuate. A pedestrian yelled. Without her knowledge, Veronica held up traffic, drowning out Shantell's voice with horns and an enraged crowd. Tugging on Shantell's arm caused tears to trickle down Shantell's face.

"I'm sorry," Veronica cried out in a panic.

She attempted to console Shantell by wiping away her tears and offering words of reassurance

"Shantell look, it's important to keep this a secret from the doctor and daddy."

CHAPTER 5

Psychiatric help

"We don't want daddy to worry, and the doctors are just looking to put mommy in the hospital. I have a lot on my mind; you understand. It's a lot of grownup stuff that has nothing to do with you, darling, so don't worry."

Shantell's actions displayed her comprehension of the situation, as she wiped away her tears before entering the doctor's office.

"Hello, may I help you?" Ask the receptionist.

"Yes, I have an appointment to see Doctor Whittman."

"And your name?"

"It's Veronica Mason."

"Ok Mrs. Mason, you can have a seat. Doctor Whittman will be with you shortly. Right now, she's finishing up with her two o'clock appointment."

"Thank you," Veronica expressing her appreciation,

Interrupted by the sight of Dr. Whittman's door opening moments later. A man, with an unsettling gaze locked onto Shantell, exited her office with visible uneasiness, raising concerns about his intentions behind seeking treatment.

"Mr. Franklin, I'll see you again next week at 2:00 pm on the dot and don't be late again," exclaimed doctor Whittman.

Mr. Franklin walked away perhaps because of the slight limp in his right leg or to let his mental projection of Shantell linger just a little longer before leaving.

"Hello Veronica, it's been a while," said doctor Whittman.

Doctor Whittman's eyes gravitated towards Shantell.

"Who do we have here?"

Extending her hand to introduce herself to Shantell. Startled by the gesture, Shantell rushed into the waiting room and assumed a defensive position on the floor, clutching her backpack.

"I'm so sorry doctor, she's still getting adjusted to things and new people but she's coming along well," explained Veronica.

"Come with me, Veronica," said Doctor Whittman. She turned to her secretary.

"Jalicia, can you keep an eye on Shantell for the duration of her mother's session?"

"Sure, not a problem. She's in excellent hands, Miss Mason, so don't worry.

Veronica sighed in relief and felt assured that Shantell would be well taken care of as she turned around and entered Doctor Whittman's office. After making sure no one was watching, Jalicia dialed the number on the phone without hesitation.

"Yeah, it's me again, now her stuck-up underpaying, you know what, thinks I'm a babysitter. She's lucky, she's, my sister. I would have already left."

Laughing due to her repetitive nature over the past few months. Struggling to remain composed, she ceased her laughter and concealed her mouth. Shantell appeared enthralled in her coloring book, as if she paid no attention to Jalicia's personal conversation but absorbed every word. Despite Shantell's seeming lack of attention, the secretary carried on with her hushed conversation.

"Do you remember that crazy lady I was telling you about who had a mental breakdown? Yeah, that's the one. She's back again, she's here now. Another session with my sister and she's adopted a little girl."

Jalicia confirmed that her own thoughts aligned with the individual she was conversing with on the phone.

"Who in their right mind would let someone that's unstable adopt a child, no matter how weird she looks?"

Despite the absurdity of Jalicia's words, Shantell

maintained a calm expression. All too familiar every time her peers and like-minded adults judged her.

"To make it even weirder," said Jalicia. She talks to herself! Yes, I understand that's a common behavior among children. Forget it, I have to use the bathroom, talk to you later."

When she hung up the phone, she maintained her interest in what Shantell was saying. She has been witnessing many children engaging in self-conversations since she began working for her sister, but this felt different. Kids, especially those without siblings, often had an imaginary friend. A rush of disconcerting emotions flooded Jalicia's mind - fear, guilt, and anxiety. Dabria leaned in, her eyes locked onto Jalicia's, and whispered in a hushed tone,

"You are cognizant of the inevitable fate awaiting you."

Dabria began chanting in a low tone, raspy voice.

"Wewe ni Kwenda kwa kuta."

Jittery, unsure of what she just heard. Filled with uncertainty, Jalicia got up and snatched her purse.

"I don't know what I just heard or what you said, but little girl! There's something wrong with you."

Jalicia barely could finish her sentence and dismissed it with a headshake.

"Hey, you just stay in that spot. I will be right back."

Jalicia exited the office and made her way across the hall. Disappearing into the lady's restroom, ensuring there was no one in sight, she entered the last stall. Certain that it would offer the privacy she required to a swift solution, disguising her efforts to regain stability has been more than challenging. Maintaining the charade, Jalicia fell back into her old habits for almost twelve months. In only a month, not able to adjust to normal rules or authority, she remained working for her sister's practice. Her sister was the sole person who could handle her obnoxious behavior, as long as she stayed clean from drugs. As she had done many times before, she hid in the stall and locked the door behind her.

While seated in the stall's privacy, she rummaged through her bag for the small container of white powder she required, aiming to confront her inner struggles with just a small dose, yet still maintain her composure and avoid arousing suspicion about her mental state. She tapped the vial against her hand, careful not to waste any, then placed her purse on the floor. Sniffing the white powder, she alternated between her left and right nostrils.

The residue blended with her pale skin as the calming hallucinogen took effect. A tranquil sensation washed over her, providing a temporary escape from the demands of reality. The peaceful moment shattered as the bathroom entrance door crashed into the wall, disturbing her serene state. Jalicia began putting things back into her purse, dropping more contents held within it than she had taken out.

"Who's there?"

Shouting nervously.

"Who's there?"

She wiped away any traces of her lack of sobriety. Once again, she asked, this time louder, about the person's identity. Again, her question remained unanswered. Then, the first bathroom stall opened and closed. Thereafter, a child giggled in the second stall, and all the faucets turned on, turning the air into mist.

"Shantell? Shantell is that you?" asked Jalicia.

A faint laugh accompanies a mix of affirmative and uncertain responses.

"You know Jalicia, the stuff you're putting in your nose is bad for you. Some may even say it could be deadly."

Jalicia attempted to free herself, banging and pushing against the stall door. Startled by the commotion, combining intoxication and panic heightened the already difficult situation. Crawling under the door was her only option. She looked through the crack beside the latch, but it was pointless. She lowered herself to the floor and stuck her head underneath, only to be kicked in her face. The impact was so quick she couldn't even get a glimpse of who was putting her through such torment as blood began dripping from her mouth and eye socket. Desperate and terrified, she retreated to the corner of the stall, her voice trembling as she cried out, begging anyone within earshot to come to her aid.

"Whoever's doing this just stop. It was an eerie moment as the bathroom lights flickered before going black. Jalicia sat there rocking back and forth, a similar feeling to the one she had before during her short-term rehabilitation process. A voice called to her.

"Jalicia? Jalicia, I know you're tired, don't you miss me?

"Mom? Jalicia called out, Mom, is that you?

The familiar voice on the other end brought comfort and nostalgia.

"Jalicia, don't you miss your mother? Don't you miss the only one who's ever understood your passion, pain, your good, and bad days? We can have that again.

"How mother? asked Jalicia. I want to know.

"Your compact Jalicia, the mirror from your makeup compact, break it and slide the glass across the scars upon both of your wrist.

Jalicia's failed suicide attempt a few years ago left her a reminder of how she viewed her life. A desolate, unfair void that robbed her of the only person who mattered. She dug in her purse and slammed the mirror from her makeup compact against the wall. Picked up a single shard of glass from the tiny pieces. she grabbed the largest one and sliced the scar tissue on both her wrists. In her desperate state, she believed that acting was her only option, finding a sense of peace in the idea of being reunited with her mother as she bled out on the bathroom floor. Jalicia drifted in and out of consciousness, her mother's soothing voice carried her back to the carefree days of her childhood. Perhaps it will be the last sound that reaches her ears.

"La La La ndio lala yangu mapenzi." Translation [Yes, sleep my love]

Soft sounds of African drums behind the sadistic child's voice. Lifeless on the floor, she will no longer awake from a sleep she has longed for. Surrounded by drug vials and other paraphernalia, the story of her life. One she had written many times before. The closing of her story's final chapter.

"So, Veronica, we're 20 minutes into our session and you haven't told me why you're here," said doctor Whittman. "You've spoken about the events in your life, which is great, thanks to Shantell's recent adoption."

"I promised my husband that I would come here. He seems to think I need to be reevaluated because of my recent episodes. I believe he's just overreacting. I may have had one or two times I have lost minutes without remembering what I said or done."

"Do you think you can elaborate?" asked Doctor Whittman. "When did this first occur?"

"I don't remember much, but it happened, and when I regained consciousness, I found broken dishes and food scattered all over the kitchen. It appeared as if a wild animal came through and ravaged everything."

"And you say you don't remember any of it?"

"Not a clue."

"Veronica, did anyone witness the episodes that you had when you blacked out?"

"Unfortunately, Shantell was there. The thought of that terrifies me to my core. I'm questioning myself now. Not knowing if I am as ready as I thought to adopt a child, especially that poor sweet little girl. God knows she's dealt with a lot, in and out of foster homes and now I bring her into our lives. I just figured I was past all this. I admit, I stopped taking my medications after we adopted Shantell."

"Your mind seems to regress to trauma, coping or denial. You blocked out your aggression shadowed by your guilt, said Doctor Whittman. To get you back on track, please resume taking your medications. And continue having our sessions at least three times a week. Also, since you say that Shantell has witnessed your episodes firsthand. I would like to speak to her next week. If you agree, I want to ensure she isn't traumatized and comprehends your experience. I believe I can help with your recovery towards you being in a better place."

Tears streamed down her face, smudging her makeup like raindrops on a windowpane.

"Veronica, why are you crying?"

Veronica's incessant sobbing and sniffles made it difficult to understand her words.

Doctor Whittman stood up and took a seat beside her. She wrapped her arms around Veronica, blanketing her with safety and comfort.

"Without fail, I carry remorse for what I did to my child every single day, and my husband's family reminds me of it. I know they deemed me sick, but it doesn't make me feel better. I thought I had moved forward as you know the adoption agency investigated my background and you vouched for me," said Veronica.

Breaking down even more, her tears couldn't dry fast enough.

"I just want to move forward, and Shantell needs stability. We need her in our lives. She completes us as a family. I, I mean we need her. If you want to see me and Shantell, we'll be here. If you don't mind me asking, do you think my husband can come with us also for the upcoming session. Perhaps more if it helped, it would make things much easier."

"Find your way by focusing on your health. After that, keeping your family together would be the easier part," said Doctor Whittman.

Amid offering comfort to Veronica, Dr. Whittman glanced at her watch.

"Well, looks like our session is over. I will have Jalicia put you guys on the schedule for next week."

Doctor Whittman looked towards Jalicia's desk and called out for her.

"Jalicia!

Shantell walked up to Doctor Whittman and her mother.

"Shantell, have you seen Jalicia? asked doctor Whittman.

"She said she would be right back and told me to stay here," said Shantell.

"Has it been long?" asked doctor Whittman.

"No, she just walked out," said Shantell.

"I can't believe she left you here alone?" said doctor Whittman. "I'm so sorry Shantell. Veronica, this is so embarrassing. I will speak to her about this."

"It's Ok, Shantell seems fine.""

"Thanks for understanding, murmured doctor Whittman. Next week, I'll see the three of you as a family."

"Mama, do I have to come back with you again? It's boring here.

Doctor Whittman reassured Shantell.

"No worries, Next time, you won't be alone I will talk to you and your mother together."

"Did I do something wrong?" asked Shantell.

"Oh no honey, it's just to talk about how happy you are at home and your new school. Sorry doctor Whittman, I don't mean to be rude, but we have to be going. It's getting late. I have to pick up dinner. I'm sure Shantell is starving by now and my husband will get off work soon. Plus, this little angel here has school tomorrow.

"I understand. Hopefully, I can locate Jalicia and close for today."

The silence during Shantell and Veronica's drive home was out of the ordinary, especially considering Shantell's chatty nature and never-ending curiosity. Veronica peered into the rearview mirror to observe Shantell's behavior. She attempted to access Shantell's mental state. So instead of her being upfront and asking Shantell if something was wrong, she chose a more subtle approach. She thought that by easing in with a different route, Shantell would be more receptive to discussing her feelings without feeling burdened.

"So, honey, what did you feel like eating for dinner?"

Despite this, Shantell sat motionless. Ignoring her mother's question, Shantell occupied herself by humming and plucking hairs from her forearm. Only her former therapist was aware that this was Shantell's coping mechanism, for situations beyond her influence. Veronica noticed Shantell seemed absorbed in her own thoughts. Letting out a sigh, Veronica whispered to herself.

"Well, I guess it's going to be pizza tonight. OK Shantell, stay in the car. I will only be a few minutes. Don't move and keep the door locked.

Shantell maintained visual contact with Veronica until she disappeared inside the building. She retrieved a blood-smeared silver charm bangle from her pocket, having removed it from Jalicia's wrist. Shantell was puzzled, unable to determine who the blood-smeared silver charm bangle belonged to. Like her time at the orphanage when she couldn't account for her actions, they accused her of being both a liar and a thief. Overwhelmed with dread at the thought of being returned to the orphanage because of her escalating incidents, she released the bracelet, watching it tumble onto the car's floor. A few minutes later, the shadows became illuminated by the sudden appearance of streetlights. A ring of lights formed around the car, casting shadows in every direction. As she observed the people encircling the car, Shantell's thoughts drifted back to the days when she felt isolated at the orphanage. Even amid a crowd, Shantell couldn't shake the feeling of solitude.

In a peculiar manner, the darkness provided her with a sense of security as the shadows turned into her companions. It was there that she sought refuge, blending into its presence. She found an escape where no one could ever ridicule her for her differences. The shadows had fulfilled their role but were now superfluous. The Masons could be the ones to guide her towards a brighter path, replacing the companions that dwelled in darkness. Veronica returned to the car.

"Sorry, that took so long." She leaned back and saw Shantell had fallen asleep. Never mind," said Veronica.

She called the house, hoping Tom would be there to spend some time together, but he didn't pick up. Veronica thought for a moment. Perhaps he's home and just didn't answer. She pulled into the vacant driveway that gave her the answers to her wandering mind. She pondered, unsure whether to call his cell phone or wait up, but then Tom sent a text. The text message read.

"Hey, honey I'm so sorry I'm going to be working late, don't wait up and give Shantell a kiss for me I will make it up to you, love you."

Each time Veronica receives a message like this from her husband, it elicits the same reactions. Veronica's mounting aggravation reached its breaking point, causing her to unleash her tears and bang on the steering wheel in a burst of frustration. The piercing scream startled Shantell from her sleep. What robbed Shantell of hope was the absence of normalcy. She had to disconnect her mind and body from her dreams, which painted a realistic picture of a life she may never experience. No one was around that showed her she could feel safe except a Swahili girl named Dabria.

Imagine a 10-year-old girl who never left outside the country that spoke Swahili to perfection. The coming and going of this persona, Dabria reared her personality, making her presence more frequent. As Shantell becomes older in age, her frustrations in her life became harder to deal with. Dabria wanted to be around forever, hence her increasing presence and Shantell's gradual disappearance. If Dabria's plan unfolds as expected, she will obliterate what remains of Shantell, making her cease to exist. The Masons were smitten with Shantell from the moment they laid eyes on her. However, their own issues remained hidden until this moment. Like previous homes, Shantell's lack of attention and turmoil were what Dabria thrived on. The evil African Swahili witch was always with her from birth.

The assumptions of doctors and close-minded, non-believers of anything hung from scientific facts. No matter what they saw or tales they heard. The nuns always monitored Shantell. They knew what doctors didn't want to admit because of their beliefs. If good can exist, why can't evil? Lacking pertinent facts, the nuns sought a psychiatrist instead of an exorcist. Once Veronica had assured Shantell that everything was fine, she took hold of the pizza and led her into the house.

"Mom, is dad going to be working late again?" Shantell asked.

"Darling, while I'm concerned, let's make sure you're taken care of, with a meal and bath before we go to sleep. Shantell focused on her meal, while upstairs Veronica gazed at her own reflection in the tub, unaware of the overflowing water pooling around her feet."

"Mommy! Mommy yelled Shantell! Veronica remained unresponsive. Shantell's increasing desperation led her to yell once more at Veronica, screaming at the top of her lungs to snap out of it. Mom, take a bath first and relax, and I will show you something I learned while in the orphanage to help you sleep better.

"No, I just need my medicine."

"Mother, once I show you this, you won't need your medicine anymore."

Shantell's gentle touch soothed Veronica's arms and hair, making her more receptive to what Shantell proposed, even if only to ease her daughter's anxiety and contribute to her mother's well-being. I'll meet you in the room after bathing and cleaning up the water. Before Shantell exits the bathroom, she passes a mirror that reveals an unnatural reflection, unclear because of condensation from the bathwater covering the mirror, making its clarity uncertain, but still resembles an adult. Shantell peered into the room where her mother was lying, awaiting her daughter's arrival. While wearing a calming smile upon her face, Shantell left, yet harboring an alternate motive in her soul. Placing candles and a few aromatics in the ideal position around her mother's bed, Shantell gathered various items around the house to create a necessary tranquility. Veronica didn't want to question Shantell's tactics. All she thought about was tranquility and mental stability, oh so she thought. Dabria's deception superseded Shantell's well-being of her mothers. Shantell rubbed her mother's temples, and Veronica went along with the idea of a remedy learned by 10-year-olds and others of her age. No matter how unwell she was feeling, Veronica's primary concern was towards Shantell's mental health.

Shantell's lips began moving, mumbling. Understood only by those who knew the Swahili language, symbolizing that Dabria was the one speaking and controlling everything Shantell was doing. Lie down Veronica, said Dabria. Veronica noticed Shantell didn't refer to her as mother but showed little concern because it's not unusual for a child to become accustomed to calling and adoptive mother or father it's such all the time, besides the fatigue and mental stress Veronica is going through made her passive about things she would normally address so she just went along with it her room smelled of Violet incense that sat in the room's corner north- south east and West followed by two candles that said above the headboard and also the foot of the bed the only lights that illuminated the room casting shadows of nothing that physically reside there the silhouettes took shapes of older relics that would be held in old Swahili in rituals possessions of the dead.

Veronica fell asleep as, Dabria stroked Veronica's hair whispering a chant increasing in volume in Swahili

"Usingizi mzito utaanguka chini ya udhibiti wangu kila ninapopigna simu [show me your sorrows, what makes you weak and most of all show me your fears]."

Dabria heard the downstairs door open, and someone was rummaging through the kitchen. She crept along the staircase and peeked over the rails.

Sounds like Tom had made it home, Tom Heard

Creaking from the loose board of the wooden floor. Dabria wasn't as light-footed as she thought. He looked around the kitchen corner calling out with a low monotone voice,

"Veronica? But no answer. Veronica, is that you? Are you up? Shantell?"

His voice echoed through the house. Tom walked up the stairs and peeked into Shantell's room. She was fast asleep, snuggling within her blankets, coddling her favorite nighttime stuffed animal. Shantell filled the room and their hearts, which were once empty. Seeking a fresh start, Tom longed to reconnect with his wife after the tragedy of their child's passing. There was still a guilt that lingered within him that made him feel he had failed. He stood there staring at the empty crib they kept in the room's corner, which he or Veronica could bring themselves to get rid of. I should have noticed something, he thought. Veronica broke down every day after giving birth and I didn't pay attention. But this time he said while pulling Shantell's blanket closer to make sure she remained warm through the night's chilly air.

All will be well. I promise, Tom thought to himself. Before exiting, he kissed her temple as a final affectionate gesture. Dabria opened her eyes when Tom exited the room. Staring with her dilated pupils tranced lopsided a blink of an eyelid. Grinning, she turned to the window, closing her eyes for the night. The next morning, a cheerful Veronica had the house smelling of homemade waffles in the air, with a memory of last night's first encounter with Dabria erased from her memory. Veronica did show signs of being more energetic, a brightness that she had lost, replenished with a perfect night's sleep.

CHAPTER 6

Fugue state

Shantell entered the kitchen, unaware of the previous night. Despite Dabria going dormant again, Shantell remains oblivious to Veronica's abnormal behavior, which comprises living a desolate life with minimal communication and lacking the motivation to accomplish more. However, Tom, who has been more observant of Veronica since her breakdown and the suspicion surrounding their child's death, could not overlook these signs.

"Morning, honey? Do you want breakfast? asked Veronica.

"Yes, please," said Shantell.

"So how did you sleep? asked Veronica, "I hope as well as I did. Oh my God, I feel so refreshed. Perhaps revisiting my doctor was just what I needed."

Dabria fed on Veronica's pain and stripped a bit of Veronica's essence the night before, unknowing to Shantell or Veronica that Dabria performed a black magic candle incantation.

Along with draining her guilt and sadness, extracting the memories of their child. Tom entered the kitchen and found it puzzling to see his wife in such high spirits. He thought it was a little premature and questioned whether his prayers had received an answer. Is this a fresh beginning for his desires? Why doubt something beneficial for his family? Shouldn't he embrace the change and the nightly prayer? Should he continue to incorporate a religious belief he grew up with but never believed in, all questions he chose not to decide on. For now, he will choose luck. Smiling, Tom moved to his wife and gave her a kiss.

"What was that for?" asked Veronica.

Laughing with joy, observing Shantell and Veronica's reactions.

"Can't a man kiss his wife?" Ask Tom.

Shantell's childish giggles of happiness and embarrassment for the second time seeing her parents kiss was amusing.

"Tom, why don't you let me bring Shantell to school this morning? I need to become more familiar with her teachers. I feel that it's time I become more involved with her activities and there's nothing like the present today will be a start. It would be another phase for them to attach to Shantell's parenting besides yours. It's time I did my part, said Veronica. I admit I've been gone for a long time. I am emotionally distanced from you, and now we have a daughter to raise. I intend to have a hand in raising her."

Tom expressed his longing for her return, which had finally come true. Tom looked over at Shantell.

"Isn't that right, Shantell?"

"Ok Tom you can go, I got this. Hurry with breakfast, Shantell, so you can get dressed for school. Don't take too long. I'll be waiting for you when you're done. I don't want you to be late on my first day bringing you there. I don't want to appear irresponsible as a parent.

As Shantell headed upstairs to get dressed for school, the phone rang. Veronica picked up the phone and answered,

"Hello? Yes, may I speak to Veronica?"

"This is she"

The trembling in her voice and constant sniffling arose Veronica's concern.

"Doctor Whittman, what's wrong?"

A momentary pause of words remained for a few seconds before she could sound out her words.

"Veronica, I apologize for calling you so early," said Doctor Whittman.

"It's OK, is there a problem?"

"It's my sister Jalicia, she's dead!"

"Oh, my God! How?"

"The police say it looks like a drug overdose, but I know it can't be true. I believe she was murdered.

"Murder!" Replied Veronica. "That's quite an accusation. What makes you believe she was murdered?"

"Well, I don't think I'm too far-fetched with this. She owed some people a lot of money from when she was using drugs. But it's not just that. I also believed she was murdered and robbed because my sister always wore a bracelet our mother gave her before she died. Jalicia never took off, and it's missing. When I found her lying dead on the bathroom floor, she didn't have it on. I asked the police if they ran across it anywhere after the autopsy. They claimed to have thoroughly searched the area and found nothing."

"Apologies, anything I can do?" asked Veronica.

"No thank you, I'm calling all my patients to reschedule appointments. Oh wait, there is one thing you can do for me. Can you ask Shantell if she saw anyone here during our session and inform me?"

"She's getting dressed for school, but I'll ask and let you know."

"And doctor Whittman, once again I am sorry for your loss."

"Thanks Veronica."

Veronica hung up the phone with a look of contempt on her face, asking herself why she should be worried about someone she knew with a coldness of Doctor Whittman's loss. Her situation improved, and Veronica's sole focus was strengthening her family bond.

"Shantell, hurry! It's time to go!" Veronica yelled. "Tom, I'm leaving to drop Shantell at school."

"Alright," said Tom, see you guys when I get home tonight.

Instead of burdening them with the news of Jalicia's death, Veronica slipped away from the house with Shantell, convincing herself of its insignificance. In some mannerism, Veronica possesses a self-centered and selfish characteristic.

"Who was on the phone, Veronica?"

But Veronica and Shantell had already pulled off heading to school. Veronica, whose usual routine didn't include school traffic, got a first- hand look at long lines and student drop offs as she looked around for a parking spot.

"Mom, you can drop me off here and I can walk into school," said Shantell.

"Maybe next time, honey, but I've never met any of your teachers and I want to introduce myself as the mother of such a beautiful little girl. Look, a parking spot!"

Her excitement diminished as another driver beat Veronica to the vacant space, reigniting the aggression that had been slowly dissipating since Dabria's initial interaction with her.

Veronica's emotions transformed into an uncontrollable rage.

"Are you insane?"

Filled with frustration, she unleashed her fury at the man who dared to park in her spot, causing chaos as everyone rushed into the school. As Veronica approached the man, Dabria's fiery temperament intensified. Witnessing the incident, Dabria reached out for Veronica's hand, absorbing her anger and helping her transition into a calm and collected state.

"What happened?" asked Veronica.

Glancing downward at Shantell and bewildered by the furious man that confronted her with anger, that stood in front of her. Mrs. Clemens rushed over to Shantell, yanking her away from Veronica, her eyes filled with concern for Shantell's safety, as well as worry about the man who was a colleague at their school.

"Shantell, are you OK?" asked Mrs. Clemens.

"Yes, this is my mom, Mrs. Clemens.

"So, you're Tom's wife?"

A bit of jealousy clouded Veronica's thoughts. Dabria yanked her hand from Mrs. Clemens and ran to Veronica.

Dabria had them playing in the precise direction, as she planned. But all this was just confrontation. Dabria needed more than just mental emotions to emerge. She devised a plan to suppress Shantell's awareness, achieving absolute control.

"No offense, Mrs. Mason, but I think we should call your husband. According to our policies, especially since we haven't seen you here to sign Shantell in or out of school before, we have to take the proper precautions. I can't release her into your care, now can you please leave the premises?

"Shantell, come with me, let's go call your father."

"Where the hell do you think you're taking my daughter?" Veronica shouted.

Dabria was still in control, instigating the entire ordeal. Dabria's voice quivered as she pleaded with Mrs. Clemens,

"I'm so scared. Please, tell me I won't have to return to the orphanage. My mom didn't mean to do what she did. She doesn't do this often."

"Shantell, what do you mean, what doesn't she do often? Did she ever hurt you?"

Dabria made sure she didn't make eye contact with Mrs. Clemens to not show misinterpretation of distress.

"She gets angry a lot and sometimes she throws things, but she's getting help, I swear," said Dabria.

"Fine, have your father pick you up. We will straighten this miss out tomorrow! exclaimed Veronica. I'm running late for an appointment that I must be at. Like Shantell said, I'm getting help with any issues I may be having. Mrs. Clemens. Perhaps I overreacted regarding the parking space."

"Regardless of how you feel about your actions, your behavior is inappropriate, and these parking spaces are reserved for staff only! said Mrs. Clemens.

Veronica looked towards the parking space in question and saw, in fact, the space was reserved for staff. Overcome with embarrassment, Veronica stammers out an apology before leaving the scene.

"Come on Shantell, let's get you to your class. I will make sure your father can pick you up after school," said Mrs. Clemens.

As Veronica made her way home, she remembered the call she had received from Doctor Whittman, realizing that her appointment had been canceled. Yet, she couldn't shake the feeling of needing to reach out and check on her. She remembered small details of last night surrounded by candles that had to be only a dream she thought to herself, but she had a vivid recollection of the intense smell of melting wax as if she was sitting enclosed within a manufacturers warehouse of smoldering candles combined with floral incense. Standing next to her was an ethereal figure of Dabria, uttering incantations in her ancestral language, Swahili, practicing the dark arts. Veronica attempts to justify the strange event, convincing herself that it originated solely from her subconscious, classifying it as a simple dream.

Just as she reached Doctor Whittman's office, her phone rang. Tom's name flashed on the screen, she let the call go unanswered. Opting not to pick up the phone, Veronica switched off her phone and made her way to the main entrance of the building, where she discovered Doctor Whitman already present, sitting with her head lowered.

"Doctor Whittman?"

Doctor Whittman raised her head teary eyed with a pale complexion expected from the of passing her sister.

"I understand that you are grieving, and I apologize for interrupting, but I wanted to make sure you were okay. I know it's tough, but any news on your sister?"

"The police are drawing their assumptions from the

fact that drugs were found on her, but I still have my own suspicions," said Doctor Whittman. My doubts will remain until they reveal the results of the autopsy. Her personal issues ended up affecting my life, which is why she started working for me. During her journey towards sobriety, she cut off ties with many people, and I feel responsible for not being able to support her.

Seeking solace, Veronica embraced Doctor Whittman despite their professional rapport.

"Listen Veronica, the detectives will need to talk to Shantell. I know she may not know anything. But if there's the slightest bit of evidence leading towards foul play, it should be known, especially with her being the last to see my sister alive. The police stated questioning everyone present is standard procedure. Although I vouched for you in a meeting, they still need your statement. I just keep thinking about my sister's bracelet. It meant so much to her that even at her lowest point of relapsing, she never exchanged it to support her habit.

"Sure! Shantell and I will come by tomorrow. Better yet, you can give the detectives my number and they can come by the house."

"Doctor Whittman admitted, "I apologize for repeating myself, but any support would greatly help."

"No problem happy to help Dr Whittman, see you soon."

With a deep sigh, she dialed Tom's number, aware of the frustration in his tone as he asked,

"Veronica, where have you been?" And why was your phone off?"

Tom was furious about what he heard regarding Veronica's behavior.

"Tom, listen, I'm sorry. I turned the phone off. I was at doctor Whittman's office.

"So, I guess after the fiasco at the school this morning you needed to see her," exclaimed Tom!

"That's not it," said Veronica. What you don't know which I would have told you before leaving the house this morning, but I was running late bringing Shantell to school, is why Doctor Whittman called the house?

Both ends of the line fell silent for a few seconds until Tom's interruption.

"Well, what did she call about? Is there something wrong with you? Did something happen during one of your sessions? She was supposed to ensure your medication regiment, which seemed effective based on your mood prior to leaving home was correct. It was a pleasant change from the norm."

"No, that was not why she called. She called because her sister is dead! Why call the house? What relevance does it hold for you? Was she sick or something? I don't understand your involvement, Tom responded."

"According to Doctor Whittman, she believes someone murdered her sister, even though it appears to be a drug overdose. She insists foul play was at hand. Shantell and I were the only ones present when her sister's missing bracelet prompted her call. Detectives require a brief conversation with Shantell and me. It's a procedure. I realize it's unlikely, but I told Doctor Whittman that Shantell might have seen someone else in the area."

'So that explains your behavior this morning at school? asked Tom." Honey, I'm so sorry for assuming you were off your medications again."

Veronica allowed Tom to express himself, accepting his assumption that her recent erratic behavior resulted from neglecting or omitting her medication.

"It would have been more considerate if you had informed me about this, considering the challenges you have already faced, involving Shantell, who has also endured a great deal. I'll be there for their questioning. This is a family situation; you and Shantell won't be dealing with it without me. So, whenever they call let me know. I can take off work if it's necessary."

Veronica succumbed to the overwhelming emotions she had been bottling up all day. Assured by her husband's comforting words, she felt a renewed sense of security in their shared journey through all their experiences.

"I'm going to head home and get some rest. I'm not feeling so good," said Veronica.

"Alright then, see you at home. I love you," said Tom.

"I love you too."

After hanging up with Veronica, Tom made another call.

"Hello, may I have a word with Mrs. Clemens?"

He figured he had to call and give some type of explanation for the behavior of his wife in a way this time retracting anything negative he may himself had said about his wife. Seeking to present a more positive perspective.

"Yes, this is Tom Mason I'm calling about this morning incident involving my wife, Veronica. You might not know her. She is Shantell's mother. The one that caused a small spectacle this morning. I'm sure that's an understatement."

"Sure, Mr. Mason, it's almost time for lunch and she's not in the office, but I will let her know you called."

"Thanks, I know she will be busy throughout the day, but I would appreciate it."

Tom checked the clock, realizing he didn't have time to wait for Mrs. Clemens to call, so he went to school. He believed a direct conversation with her would be more effective in addressing the issue seriously. Since Shantell was new to the school, Tom emphasized the importance of stability for her adoption. Tom drives up to the school and walks into the office, where Mrs. Clemens is preparing to enjoy her lunch.

"I'm so sorry to disturb your lunchtime. I can wait outside for you to finish, but I felt an urgent need to be here and explain my wife's actions with no consequences, especially given Shantell's placement."

"Not being too eager about my lunch today, Mr. Mason, I wasn't enthusiastic about it, to be honest. It's not like I had anything delicious anyway, just a salad, you know. I'm on a diet, so believe me, you saved me from having to consume these leafy greens that some people consider a meal. Unfortunately, there's a big high school reunion, or should I say my big high school reunion coming up soon and I'm trying to look my best to impress my old classmates."

"If it helps at all, I don't think that impressing anyone of your past classmates would be an issue. You look fine to me. Mrs. Clemens blushed at Tom's compliments. He made her day, unaware of its significance."

"Tom, let's pretend like this morning never even occurred, okay? I'll address concerns in our next meeting, regarding personal issues. I'm sure it won't happen again."

Mrs. Clemens, oblivious remarked

"Is that right?"

"Oh no Mrs. Clemens, it won't."

Tom's ignorance made him unaware that he may have sent flirtatious innuendos towards her.

"So, how is your wife doing? Between you and me, for her to be taking care of Shantell without you watching her every move?"

"Yes, she's doing well for now, despite the temporary nature of the situation."

He turned around and there stood Miss. Sanchez.

"Hello, Tom."

"Francine, how are you doing today? I'm here to apologize for my wife's disturbance this morning."

"Oh yeah, Miss. Sanchez remarked.

Her voice filled with contentment as she appreciated being addressed correctly. Which made Tom chuckle, his skin turned a blushing bright red.

"I have it from here, Mrs. Clemens," said Francine.

You may return to your classroom. I'm sure they're getting antsy and on the verge of being disruptive."

"You're right, let me get back to the little animals. Oh my gosh, I'm so sorry Tom. I didn't mean animals, of course. I'm sounding so crazy right now with how I'm speaking. Sometimes when I leave the classroom too long, it's like a zoo, they're jumping everywhere throwing papers, pencils, and books, so on and so forth. explained Mrs. Clemens."

"That's alright, I know what you mean, and I know you guys have your hands full of these students and all you needed was that extra from my wife this morning. I'll be seeing you later Mrs. Clemens hopefully under better circumstances," said Tom.

"I don't mean to overstep Tom, and I know it's none of my business. You don't have to answer, but what sort of problems are you and your wife having? I mean, considering how well put together you seem to be. I wouldn't imagine that it could be marital issues. I promise whatever the reason, it will go no further than you and me," said Miss Sanchez. Trying to find out information about the strength of their marital situation discreetly as possible.

"No, I don't mind speaking to you about it I needed to speak to someone I thought I had it all together, but it's just been too much to carry on my own."

Tom seemed clueless to her intentions but from the outside looking in on both parts there seemed to be a connection, whether it was physical or mental, wasn't set in stone.

"It's just for me to know," said Miss Sanchez, so I can understand how to tread with Shantell in case she needs extra attention. Tom, you do not know how many students I deal with regularly. Each student facing family issues that hinder their learning capabilities is a one-of-a-kind case, so handle each situation with utmost care. Adults often overlook the fragile minds of the young. Many feel it's essential to dedicate 75% of your attention to the child in family situations. And it's the complete opposite. It's paying attention to their parents or caregivers contrary to disbelief most of the teachings come from home. As teachers which I also consider myself, despite what my diploma says as a counselor, we are all teachers.

Tom acknowledged that his conversation with Francine was truly captivating.

"It would be pleasurable to listen to you all day, but I have to be going.

"Who claimed it needed to last the entire day? "Perhaps we can find a few minutes soon to speak one-on-one," said Francine.

Muffling her laughter so that it wouldn't echo through the school halls.

"Parents should get acquainted when their kids meet, trust is crucial. Believe me, I understand you don't have to tell me twice. In fact, why don't you write my cell phone number just in case. You know in case there's something you may need regarding Shantell, of course." said Francine.

"You can just tell me I have a photographic memory trick of the trade," replied Tom.

"So, you won't forget this entire conversation we've had? asked Francine.

"Not at all," said Tom.

But before I give you my number, I want to ask you. How do you feel about Shantell coming over to my house for my daughter's slumber party this weekend? Shantell has been shaken since this morning. She asked me to talk to you about a slumber party with her female classmates at my house.

"You know if I had to answer now, it would be a definite yes, but I must include my wife's opinion, I'm sure she would agree especially with Shantell making new friends. Which will show growth with her personality, with my fingers crossed of course. Well, OK Francine, I'm sure I've taken enough of your time, and I have a few errands to run as usual. I'm a busy guy. I will allow you to do your counseling and teaching duties, and we can discuss the sleepover later."

Overwhelmed with happiness, Tom stepped back, his smile grew wider. He forgot about the ongoing issues with Veronica and Shantell and the impending conversation with the investigators.

"Wait a minute Sir!

Miss. Sanchez leaned in a seductive tone.

"Didn't you forget something?

"I don't think so," Tom said. I told you I have a photographic memory, especially for important matters.

"My phone number, remember? asked Francine.

"Oh yeah, it slipped my mind! I got so absorbed in the conversation that I forgot about it.

"Are you certain you don't want to write it down?

"Nope, I'm hanging on to your every word. Go ahead.

"OK it's (475) 276-3417, you got it?

"Yes, I do, now let me test your memory," said Tom.

"So, the very first day that I brought Shantell into school, what color shirt was I wearing?

If I remember correctly, your outfit comprised a button-up collared shirt in navy-blue, a tie in black and burgundy, a blue blazer, and navy-blue pants.

Francine exuded confidence as she stood with her arms crossed, her finger pointed to her temple in deep concentration.

Wow, that is impressive," said Tom.

"Ok Mr. Mason, last question, can repeat my number back to me?

"475-276-3417, Tom responded.

"Sheesh what an amazing mind you have among other things that I've noticed, lock in my number and I will get back with you before the end of the day and let you know about the sleepover. In fact, text me your number so I can give you that information as soon as possible, makes little sense for you to have my number when I am supposed to call you with an answer."

"Not a problem," said Tom. I'll text it to you, I hope to see you later."

After a supposed brief interaction turning into casual conversation, they finally part ways. Tom trusts the intended matter will be handled appropriately. Upon entering his car Tom's phone rings again with Veronica on the other end but this time he picked up the call,

"Hello Tom? Where have you been?"

"I was at Shantell's school trying to fix the mess you made. Veronica, what's wrong with you? Did you even consider how your actions would affect Shantell?"

Remorse replaced Veronica's desire for an answer from Tom as she realized the impact her actions had on Shantell, rendering her speechless. When roles reverse and pressure mounts, how can she answer the unknown?

"Tom, I don't know. Everything around me seemed to move at an accelerated rate. I had an overwhelming feeling as though everyone was attacking me, and I became defensive."

"It sounds as though you're getting worse. What is Dr. Whittman's opinion on your recent experiences? Perhaps you should see a doctor, your condition appears to be worsening."

"Wait Tom, said Veronica in desperation. I have to be honest about the medications Dr. Whittman prescribed for me. I haven't been taking them."

"What! exclaimed Tom, "Why? That's the main reason you returned to see Dr. Whittman."

You can hear the anger and disappointment in his voice. Neglecting to disclose any mention of medications to her psychologist, Veronica had just added another fabrication to an extensive collection of falsehoods she had already constructed. Confronted with the possibility of falling apart, Veronica had to acknowledge that she believed she had a firm grip on her life.

"I hate to monitor you, Veronica, but it's necessary to make sure you're taking your medication because your selfishness is affecting both me and Shantell."

"Tom, I agree if it's best for our family. I have more than enough resources that I haven't been using. I now have a family and I will reach out to the meetings that Dr. Whittman suggested me joining. But can we talk more about it later, someone's at the door?"

"Ok, that sounds fine. Let's address this later. Remember, we care about you and want to support you with compassion, love, and understanding."

"Tom, the detectives called. They plan to visit later today at 5 o'clock. Can you pick up Shantell and come on time for their questions? Veronica expressed her reluctance to deal with the situation.

"There's nothing to worry about Tom quickly reassured her. Keep in mind these questions are just a formality to cover all their bases. It's their job besides you were in your session and Shantell already said she didn't see anything. The statement they have included in their investigation has to be verified in person.

"But Tom, she's just a child. This is not how I imagined Shantell's new life with us."

"Shantell is stronger than you think Veronica, she's a bright girl. I'm sure with the explanations we give her of why she's being questioned, she'll understand, which I will further explain to her when I pick her up from school. I'll put in extra hours, get Shantell, and go home. To meet the Monday deadline, I'll work from home all weekend, so I'll be busy."

Veronica's disappointment was evident as she revealed her plan of taking Shantell to the aquarium as a surprise.

"Listen honey, I'm sorry but you know since you stopped working my income is the only one for the entire household, add the medical bills plus the therapist and medications etc. makes it extremely difficult for me to be frivolous with the time I put into work. Besides, I forgot to mention that Shantell will be with some classmates who invited her to a sleepover this weekend. I will drop her off after we speak to the detectives."

"I assume you forgot Shantell has two parents, not just a father. You chose not to even ask me first," said Veronica.

"I was going to mention it to you, but the subject slipped my mind. When we began speaking about the school incident and you taking not your prescriptions, which have you taken them today?"

"Yes, I have," said Veronica.

"I don't have a choice but to believe you this time. Take them in the morning so I can witness it firsthand."

"You realize you can't watch me twenty-four hours a day, right?"

"Yeah," sighed Tom, we cross that bridge when that time comes. Look, I have to go now go now. We will speak later."

In a display of annoyance, Veronica slammed her phone on the table, resulting in a cracked screen, all without uttering a farewell. She failed to recognize that her recent actions left Tom with no other option but to decide based on her behavior, despite his passivity in other matters.

Veronica gazed at her purse before retrieving her medication for depression and anxiety. In her mind, if her prescribed dosages are minimum at best, she should be able to double the amounts with no issues.

Yearning to fulfill her role as a mother and wife, she consumed them one after another. In a single swallow, she ingested the equivalent of two days' medication: 120 mg duloxetine and 2 mg clonazepam per day. This was more than her body was used to, especially now since she wasn't taking them, not giving her body time to acclimate to the pills. Instantly, she felt the powerful effects, a deep calmness enveloping her, accompanied by a blissful euphoria. Fueled by a surge of motivation.

Veronica tackled all her household tasks, leaving no corner untouched. She achieved more in a few hours than her typical couple of days' worth. Sweating heavily, she glanced at her watch and realized she had underestimated the passing of time.

Oblivious to the detectives' imminent arrival, Veronica quickly ran upstairs for a brief shower. As soon as she stepped under the running water, her phone broke the silence with its insistent ringing. The sound of rushing water drowned out Tom's attempted phone call. Tom remained seated in his car, stationed in front of Shantell's school, ready to pick her up. Wanting to make sure his wife's needs were met before they headed home, he tried to call her, but as expected, she did not answer. A sudden knock on his window startled him, causing him to look up and see Miss. Sanchez standing there with a huge smile on her face.

Observing Sanchez's beaming smile, Tom rolled down his window and remarked.

"Looks like someone had an incredible day!" Why do you say that?" laughed Miss. Sanchez?

"I'm just going by the smile and facial expressions. Honestly, Tom, it was just an ordinary tiring day. My day didn't get better until now."

Subtly hinting, that he brought out her smile.

"I just wanted to remind you of the sleepover tonight.

"I remembered," said Tom, and I mentioned it to my wife, so I should drop her off around seven o'clock, give or take. There are tasks to handle before she arrives.

"No, that's perfect, with excitement Miss. Sanchez mentioned the requirement was for all girls to be present by six. I'll speak formally to parents, then set out snacks for girls before they get ready to have fun."

"Alright, we'll speak later tonight, Francine, Goodbye."

"Bye Tom,"

"I forgot to ask you how your day went," said Tom to Shantell.

"It was ok, but I still need help with math."

"We'll review it to catch you up on your next assignment. However, I have a surprise for you. I want you to meet someone before we head home."

"Who is it," asked Shantell?

"Wait and see."

"And don't worry, we'll return to meet mom and speak with the detective."

"But what about?"

Shantell attempted to say something, but Tom's interruption swiftly halted her words.

"And yes, you can and will make it to your friend's party."

Shantell's enthusiasm brought a smile to Tom's face, and he laughed. The mention of a surprise, which typically entailed personalized gifts that would be advantageous to her, immediately sparked Shantell's interest.

CHAPTER 7

Hello grandma!

They arrived at the Robinson medical retirement home where Tom's mother stayed.

"Dad is this where my surprise is?" asked Shantell.

"Yes, I want you to meet my mother, who is now your grandmother. She and I haven't had the best connection, but I love her and want you to meet her. Now, anytime you feel uncomfortable speaking to her, tell me and we will leave, no questions asked. So, are you ready to head inside?

With a hint of uncertainty, Shantell replied.

"I suppose I'm ready."

"My mother has a medical condition called

Alzheimer's. I'm not sure if you know what that means, but I will explain it to you later. Let's go make it happen."

They approached the nurses' station to sign in.

"Hello, I'm here to see my mother, Anna Mason."

"Sure, and you are?"

"Her son, Tom Mason."

"Ok Mr. Mason, you can go right down the hall to her room. The staff should have fed and cleaned her for the day."

"We appreciate your help, Nurse Tamara," said Tom."

Making their way down the corridor where his mother's room was, it appeared as if he was an inmate on his last day towards death row. Tom's nerves were on edge, not due to his own circumstances, but out of concern for Shantell. The negative environment he had grown up in had left him numb, and he made a promise to himself that if he ever started a family, he would foster a one-of-a-kind atmosphere for his child. To avoid disturbing his mother, Tom peered into her room before Shantell followed him inside, calling out.

"Mom? Tom whispered quietly."

As Shantell trailed behind Tom, attempting to stay inconspicuous, his murmured words echoed in her mind. Shifting her attention to the door where they had been standing moments ago, Tom's mother peered out the window. The piercing sunlight revealed a glimpse of her hidden emotions, a heart that had grown cold yet still held a flicker of warmth within.

"Hey mom, do you recognize me?"

Despite Tom's attempt to trigger a memory by reminding his mother of a shared moment, she remained silent, leaving him with a sense of disappointment and longing for recognition.

"It's me, Tom, your son. I brought someone here to visit you." Tom eased Shantell in front of him so his mother could get a clearer look."

Her name is Shantell, your granddaughter, Veronica, and I adopted her. She is part of our family.

As Tom's mother moved her lips to utter something, the silence persisted. Tom then turned to Shantell and inquired if she wished to say hello to her grandmother. Shantell stepped forward to become inches away from her grandmother's bedside, hello said Shantell with an eager look upon her face. Her nervousness faded quickly once introduced to her. Tom's mother averted her gaze from Shantell and focused on the view outside, leaving Shantell and Tom feeling rejected.

"Remember what I told you about my mom being ill before we left the car? Well, that's what's happening now. She just needs a moment to adjust to having a beautiful new granddaughter."

"I understand," said Shantell."

"Shantell, take this opportunity to familiarize yourselves, while I grab drinks. How does that sound?"

"Sounds OK, I'll be fine. I will continue to try speaking to my grandmother until you get back."

"OK honey yes you need me just holler down the hall more if you can remember how to get to the nurses station you can ask them to call for me over the intercom."

With Tom gone, Shantell moved across the room to the other side of her grandmother's bed, where she could also see the window that had captured her grandmother's gaze. With her eyes locked onto her grandmother's face, Shantell inched closer, and the silence that had hung in the air since they arrived dissipated when Tom's mother uttered a single word: pickaninny. Shantell's eyes widened and watery with disbelief as she struggled to comprehend the meaning behind Tom's mother's words, unintentionally giving Dabria the advantage once again.

Dabria peeked out of the room door, ensuring Tom's absence, and closed it. She hurriedly walked towards Tom's mother and grabbed her head, squeezing tightly, causing his mother's eyes to tear up because of pain inflicted by Dabria and into her ear Dabria whispered.

"I am going to kill your old wrinkled white ass."

Dabria removed the safety pin from her school's name tag, planning to use it as a tool to puncture a hole in the breathing tube of Tom's mother.

"You see Shantell, no one will ever mess with you while I'm around and I'm not going anywhere," said Dabria."

In that moment, Dabria's departure left Shantell overwhelmed by the negative emotions stirred by her grandmother's words, prompting her to rush to her father and express her desire to leave.

No questions asked to his mother, figuring he himself would only just get silence. Tom figured the mother that he grew up knowing paid a visit to Shantell while he was out of the room, unable to defend her. Tom thought to himself that his mother's disease was all a facade. He firmly believed that she exhibited an unapologetic demeanor for her consistent mistreatment towards him. Especially now, since he has adopted an African American daughter into their family.

Tom and Blair's parents were pure of white Catholic blood, but what history has shown is that ignorance has an ugly head because no one is a genuine pure blood, especially not in America. Tom wanted to tell his mother that he loved her despite her ignorance. But the tears in his daughters' eyes washed away any possibility of reconciliation with her or having a relationship with Shantell.

"Let's go Shantell your grandmother needs her rest Tom paused, honey can you give me a second and wait in the hall while I say goodbye to my mother?"

Shantell glanced at Tom's mom before leaving the room. Tom approached his mother, ensuring Shantell was out of earshot, and leaned in to speak to her.

"You know mother, Tom whispered into her ear despite growing up and being subjected to your bigotry, being ostracized, and passed on to live with Blair because I didn't agree with how you and dad wanted me to live, I still love you but know when you leave this earth I may shed a tear, I may not either way my life will go on and I plan on it being a happy one. Tom bid his mother farewell with a kiss on her forehead, stating, "It's your loss" before parting ways.

As he left his mother's room. Tom felt a wave

of sadness wash over him, and he couldn't help but notice the troubled expression on Shantell's face, leading him to suspect that she might have overheard his conversation with his mother, despite his efforts to prevent it. Considering the possibility that she had heard; he changed the subject to something more cheerful to reassure her.

"So, honey, are you ready to have your very first sleepover? It should be a ton of fun. Ummu, I believe so," said Shantell. I'm eager at the same time.

Tom's comforting action of wrapping his arm around Shantell's shoulder conveyed his message of unwavering support.

"Miss. Sanchez is a nice person, and you already are friends with her daughter, right?"

"I suppose," with a tone of despair.

In that instant, Shantell's demeanor took on a brighter and more joyful disposition. But Dabria's anger had been festering, merging Shantell's soul with negativity and maliciousness. However, circumstances appear to be working against her devious intentions, with the goal of seizing full authority over the body and eradicating Shantell's awareness. One step forward for Dabria was short-lived by so much positivity that her parents kept countering with the negative. Dabria believed it was time to intensify.

"Ok Baby girl let's head home," said Tom. With frustration clear in his voice.

CHAPTER 8

I feel fine

Veronica, sleeping in the bathtub, woke to the doorbell. She glanced at her timepiece and leaped out of the tub, comprehending that the clock had already struck 5, and now a few minutes had passed, leaving her still undressed. In a frenzy, she wrapped herself in a bathrobe and dashed downstairs to open the door.

"Who is it?" asked Veronica. Before she looked through the peephole.

"It's detective Joseph Chase with the Connecticut police department. Could I speak to Mrs. Veronica mason? She's expecting me."

"Oh, of course, the detective. Give me a few minutes to get dressed. Damn!"

Veronica, realizing Tom wasn't even home yet, rushed to her phone and started dialing. Tom answered the phone at the exact moment Veronica was dialing his number to inform him of her delay.

"Hello, Tom, where are you? The detective is here."

"We're on our way. Don't worry, we should be there in five minutes."

"Ok, can you please hurry? Shantell should be here to answer the questions, but it won't be a problem for me to address any concerns he has."

Right after hanging up, Veronica raced upstairs to get dressed, fixing her hair and make-up to make herself presentable. Enough, she said, as she finished her hair and looked in the mirror. Taking longer than she expected to get ready, Veronica almost forgot that the detective was still standing outside, waiting for her to let him in. Veronica's heavy breathing accompanied her opening the door, her voice echoing,

"Hold on, detective, I'm coming,"

The detective's persistent knocking intensified. Until Veronica answered the door.

"Did I catch you at a bad time," asked detective Chase?

"I was in the bathroom when you arrived, so I'm behind on my tasks."

"Sorry for the interruption, but I need answers urgently because of unforeseen circumstances. Is your daughter here also?"

"Not yet, my husband just picked her up from school. They'll be here shortly. Any further case inquiries or updates on leads or new information?"

"I can't share details about the case unless you're a victim's family member, but we now believe it was a homicide."

"Sure, detective, I understand. While we're waiting, may I offer you something to drink? What about coffee, tea, or cold lemonade to drink?"

"I would accept a glass of scotch when I'm off duty, but coffee would be fine. I require caffeine. This case keeps me awake and restless."

"Are you sure it's the case and not the caffeine that's keeping you awake at night? asked Veronica. I had similar sleep issues, but reducing caffeine helped me sleep better."

Veronica used casual conversation as a delay tactic until Tom and Shantell showed up, even though she fabricated her claim about sleeplessness.

"Maybe I'll switch to decaf later, but for now, caffeinated coffee is fine."

"Sure, I will be right back."

In Veronica's absence, detective Chase capitalized on the moment to peruse a few images, aiming to gain insights into the dynamics within the family. No pictures of Shantell, except for a single image of a baby boy, very young.

"Here you go detective, I didn't know if you wanted cream or sugar with your coffee, so I brought both."

"Straight black is fine, Mrs. Mason, thank you."

"I noticed you don't have pictures of your daughter here, but a boy, excuse me for assumptions which I only assume because of the color clothing the child is wearing and the type of toys in the background."

"Wow detective you're very observant, yes that was our son he passed away not long after he was born, concluded as cradle death I'm still dealing with, I'm not all the way there but with adopting Shantell I'm learning to move forward."

"Sorry for your loss, but if you don't mind me asking. Is that the reason you're seeing Dr. Whittman?"

"Not to go into details, but yes, she's helping me deal with the grieving aspect of my son's death."

"And your husband, how is he dealing with the loss?"

"You can ask him yourself when he arrives. I can't answer for him. Some people handle grief better or worse than others."

Shantell and Tom arrived, greeting Veronica at the door handling moments after the sound of two car doors slamming. Tom and Shantell entered the house with smiles on their faces.

"How was your day, Shantell? Veronica asked?"

"It was ok mommy; can I have a snack now?"

"Sure honey, after you speak to Mr. Chase first."

Shantell was disappointed having to veer away from her normal after-school snack. Detective Chase noticed the disappointment on Shantell's face and reassured Mrs. Mason that there was no need to hurry.

"I'm so sorry. Where are my manners, detective? This is my husband, Tom."

The detective extended his hand to Tom. Tom wasn't as eager to show the same etiquette before seeing Veronica's side eye and obvious embarrassment. They interlocked their hands with a tight grip. Tom, with unwavering determination, made it unmistakably clear that he would not be cowed or frightened when it came to defending his family.

"Guys, I'm going into the kitchen to give this impatient young lady her snack. Tom, do you want anything?"

"No honey thanks, I'm just going to keep the detective company until you get back."

Tom sat in his recliner, arms folded, beside the detective. He inquired, "What do you need to ask my daughter?"

"I need Shantell to recount what she remembers about the day Jalicia Whittman was found dead.

Can you tell me why she has to continue dwelling on such a traumatic memory?

"Weren't those questions already answered by her? No second chances for what you seek from her. So, I'm going to ask you to leave," said Tom."

"I will respect your wishes Mr. Mason but know that this doesn't make things easier on your behalf."

"Bye detective," said Tom. We're done."

Moments after detective Chase left the Mason's, the home phone rang. Hello?" answered Tom.

"Tom, it's Blair, I have some bad news. Mom passed

away. I received the call from the facility a few minutes ago." Tom stood there mute in disbelief. Despite the gray areas he had with his parents, he still loved them hold heartedly and the tears that ran down his face showed it.

"Tom, can you meet me there. Considering you oversee all her paperwork. I wouldn't be able to make any decisions regarding her belongings."

"Blair I already know, and even if I wasn't responsible for her belongings I can't let you take care of this alone. We must support one another, and with mom's passing, I've gained clarity. I believe we need to start on a clean slate, life is too short. Tom said, "Family is all we have."

"I agree little brother, I love you, and I'll see you there."

CHAPTER 9

Hell has frozen over

Dabria sat downstairs, not in the slightest breaking the role she now needed to play indefinitely. But in a way, the Masons wouldn't suspect or question any obscure characteristics. She sat there with Shantell's favorite doll brushing its hair while humming a cheerful tune. Heightening her eagerness to leave to attend the sleepover, she had to reassure the Mason's that their daughter didn't hear the conversation. Dabria's excitement to play with Shantell's peers for an entire weekend without her parents around left them clueless to what may come.

"Shantell, you look like you're ready to leave," said Tom.

"Yep, dad, I'm so eager."

"Let's go."

"No honey, mommy will bring you. Daddy has to go meet your aunt Blair. She needs him to help her with something."

"Can't mom help Aunt Blair?" asked Dabria.

Continuing to push a wedge between Tom and Veronica with her antics to keep Veronica out of the parental loop. She knew that this would continue to drive Veronica mad.

"What's wrong with me bringing you?" asked Veronica.

Her voice filled with disappointment and her face displaying discouragement. Perplexed, she failed to understand why her cherished daughter, whom she had grown to adore and believed she had a close bond with, had such difficulty with her leaving her at the slumber party.

"Nothing!" said Dabria.

Adding intensity to her voice. But not so much that Tom and Veronica suspect her as the one with an issue. Dabria wanted to give a few nudges towards Veronica, to question herself as a parent. Tom's continuous exclusion of her from decisions may have influenced her thoughts.

"Shantell, it's fine for mom to take you there, as long as you arrive, right? The longer we talk about who brings you will be the shorter the amount of time you could spend with your friends now, explained Tom. So, are you ok with mom taking you? I promise I will call to check on you when I'm done helping Aunt Blair, ok?

"Ok," said Dabria.

"Shantell, let go," said Veronica

Who decided not to make a big issue about Shantell's abrupt change with having a problem with her wanting to do things alongside her without the presence of her father. Veronica convinced herself that maybe she has been pushing too hard and Shantell's adjustment is still taking its delicate course and from what she has always heard was that girls tend to gravitate more towards their father anyway as she did herself when she was a child.

"Ok, I've decided," Tom said." Mom will be the one bringing you to where you will have the most fun you have ever had."

Figuring that Shantell reluctance that she be dropped off by anyone but him was probably because she looked at him as her protector, though she didn't verbally express her thoughts about it.

"Do you think you can do me a favor and let me use your car? My vehicle has been making an odd sound lately, and I don't want to risk getting stuck with Shantell. I apologize for not mentioning it earlier, but we have been incredibly busy, and I overlooked it."

"Alright you guys can take my car," said Tom. "It's too late to bring it to the shop, but tomorrow I believe the auto shop that I normally go to will be open. If not, first thing Monday morning I'll bring it in. I just hope it's nothing serious and I make it to work before lunch." Dabria cried out, intentionally interrupting. Surreptitiously grinding into their relationship.

"Can we go now?"

"Ok, ok let us go now before this lil lady explodes," said Veronica.

Tom heard the noise mentioned by Veronica about her car as he left the driveway. He prayed for the car to last through the weekend, with Veronica and Dabria following him. Veronica turned off onto a side road in the opposite direction to Miss. Sanchez house, although still concerned about Tom's mentality of him having to drive under emotional distress because of the loss of his mother on top of driving her car that continued to roll in an unpredictable capacity. Her focus was on one task at a time.

To avoid accidents, she must keep her thoughts on the road. Veronica started a conversation with her daughter, to try finding that connection that she thought they were creating.

"Honey, do you think you will get along with the girls at the party?" asked Veronica.

Just throwing a random question out there to break the silence. Dabria sat in the back seat, deliberately ignoring Veronica to elicit a response.

"I want nothing more than for you and me to have a close relationship. That means you can speak to me about anything good or bad."

Dabria gave Veronica just a little, only enough to play puppeteer, to Veronica's depression an illness she was finally getting a handle on, so she thought.

"I know Veronica," said Dabria. I guess I just have to spend more time with you. Daddy has done a lot for me. I just got used to him being around and talking to him about everything!"

Dabria played astutely, putting much more emphasis on some keywords than others did so that they didn't fly over Veronica's head. Veronica fell silent, and Dabria knew her few words had wounded her more than physical pain would. But Veronica remained focused, not at any point showing how Dabrias' words had affected her outwardly as much as it did inwardly. Small droplets of salty water covered Veronica's collared shirt but evaporated just-in-time, right before pulling into Miss. Sanchez's driveway.

"We're here, grab your bag and I will walk you to the door."

But before they could exit the vehicle, miss. Sanchez was coming out of her house and directed a sarcastic greeting towards Veronica. Miss. Sanchez thought she had masked her expressions well, but it was noticeable. Veronica suspected the temporary unhinging in the school's parking lot caused the awkwardness. But that wasn't it at all. Francine was disappointed because she couldn't continue the conversation with Tom. Which she had enjoyed immensely.

"Hello again Mrs. Mason," said Miss. Sanchez kindly.

"Hello, thank you for inviting Shantell to sleep over. This is exactly what she needs.

"No need to thank me. My daughter loves her and

I'm sure she and the other girls will get along just fine. I treat all my students as if they were my own. Thank you. I see I'm leaving her in excellent hands."

"Hey there, Shantell, are you ready to meet the girls?" asked Miss. Sanchez.

"I sure am," said Dabria.

"Ok let's go, wait can we talk for a minute," asked Veronica?

"Sure, umm Shantell, why don't you go inside and meet the girls? They should be in the kitchen making snacks. Just help yourself. I'll be inside momentarily."

"Yes ma'am," said Dabria. Quickly bolting off towards the house.

Veronica shouted "Honey, aren't you going to give me a hug before you go?"

Dabria didn't even look back even though she heard Veronica's obvious cry for affection she purposely disregarded, a reaction that was noticeable by Miss. Sanchez being a mother herself but didn't address.

"Miss. Sanchez, I'm sure you noticed the cold shoulder I received from Shantell. I believe it's related to the school incident, and that's what I wanted to discuss with you. I figured I owed you, among others an apology."

Miss. Sanchez stood there, with her arms tightly crossed. Witnessing firsthand the explosive nature of Veronica's outbursts, and that's putting it lightly. But to not escalate anything, Miss. Sanchez assured Veronica that she had already smoothed things over with the school staff. As for herself, she had already resolved the issue and offered words of advice regarding Shantell, explaining that her reaction was an involuntary response after many years of being a teacher.

"Veronica, I won't attempt to dictate your parenting choices. As someone who has worked with numerous children over the years, I understand that parenting is a continuous learning process. It can be a sensitive topic, especially if there are factors causing household instability."

"What do you know about anything happening in my home? asked Veronica. You know what never mind, she exclaimed I'm here to make amends and start on a new slate."

"You're right Mrs. Mason and I apologize if I was out of line and for our kids' sake. They enjoy spending time together, seeing each other at school, they're almost inseparable. It's an amazing thing although Melanie is friends with the girls inside already, she struggled to connect with any of them, that is until your daughter came along."

"I appreciate you hearing me out and accepting my apology, let me leave you to this amazing experience with these group of girls that will be pumped up with lots of sugar before the end of the night." They both laughed out loud, "Well good night and good luck." laughed Veronica as she walked away to enter her car and drove off.

CHAPTER 10

The sleepover

Miss. Sanchez walked into her house, and as expected, it was a circus inside six little sugar-filled girls climbing walls, slightly chaotic, everyone except Dabria. Francine walked up to her daughter and pulled her to the side.

"Melanie, please ensure Shantell feels welcome by engaging with her in all the games. In fact, did you introduce your other friends to Shantell?"

"Not exactly," Melanie responded. "Shantell mentioned she didn't know how to play the game and would watch until she figured it out."

"Ok Melanie, do you or your friends need anything right now?"

Melanie suggested having more popcorn, but she recommended taking baths before snacking. "Girls gather around, I'll introduce you to someone new. This is Shantell. Newly arrived, she attends school with Melanie and me. I believe only two of you are unfamiliar with Shantell. All the others already attend school with them. Brittney's right side is occupied by Carla, who stands next to Shantell. Amber, to Melanie's left, bears a resemblance to Carla as they are sisters. With the introductions out of the way, Melanie, as you have already finished bathing, why don't you escort them upstairs so they can grab their pajamas and take turns freshening up? Once everyone finishes, I have a surprise in store for all of you."

CHAPTER 11

Foul Play

Tom's drove to the rest home where his mom stayed before her recent death was a difficult one, not one of what you may think considering the situation but one of his journey to get there and also about making it to retirement home to finalize paperwork to have his mother's body released to the coroners due to him holding the power of attorney with important decision making involving his mother, but in order to do so he first had to pray that he didn't get stranded on the back roads he used as a shortcut. The knocking of Veronica's car engine kept getting louder and the smell of melting rubber began coming from the air vents. Tom parked and turned off the engine. He reached into the side pockets of the front seat, where he had placed an emergency flashlight. With successful difficulty grabbing hold of the light, he lost his grip, and the flashlight slipped and rolled onto the back floor. Toms' frustration started to build, dammit Tom shouted, before pulling on the door handle to exit the car to retrieve the flashlight on the rear floor, using only the sense of feel because where he was didn't have any streetlights and the moon didn't illuminate as it usually does on a less cloudy night.

While searching for the flashlight, Tom pulled out all kinds of trash left behind by Shantell, which included candy wrappers, half eaten bags of chips, etc. Tom grabbed the flashlight and began pulling it out, but clinging to it was a circular metal object. Once he could shine a light on it, the object became clearer. It was a silver bangle bracelet. Tom figured it belonged to Veronica, so he just threw it into the cupholder. He turned on the flashlight, being relieved that it still worked. He popped open the hood with hopes he could fix the problem that was causing the car to smoke. Tom moved wires around, knowing he wasn't versed in automotive mechanics. He tried before seeking help, being prideful, hating the idea of someone fixing a loose wire and making him appear ignorant.

After about 15 minutes of not making any progress, Tom called his sister to see if she was still with their mother so he could inform them of his predicament. Figuring that maybe the doctors would allow his sister to sign all the paperwork if he granted permission.

Being stranded in a remote area made getting reception difficult, so he had to climb a nearby hill to make a call. Blair wasn't picking up her phone, so he tried calling the nursing station and got an answer.

"Hello," said the night shift nurse.

"Hello, I'm Tom Mason. I'm not sure if you may know, but my mother passed away tonight, and my sister was supposed to have made it there. Her name is Blair. Do you know if she's there," Tom asked?

"Yes, she is." The nurse responded. "We were just here getting the paper ready for your arrival."

"Well, I ran into a problem and won't be able to sign the paperwork. If I allow my sister to handle the papers, would it cause any problems?"

"Sorry, Mr. Mason, that wouldn't be a question I would be at liberty to answer. I'll verify to make sure it's not an issue."

"Could you hold on for a minute?

"Sure," said Tom.

Shortly, the nurse returned to the phone, while Tom stayed on hold. "Mr. Mason?"

"Yes."

"Well, Mr. Mason, my supervisor said it would be fine since you're the one who's giving your sister that responsibility if she is willing to do so."

"Another consideration is that I haven't had a chance to let her know: could you please pass on the message for her to contact me, or would you prefer to transfer the call now for convenience?

"Of course, I can contact her through the phone. Please wait a moment while I locate her."

The temperature dropped lower, chilling Tom's core through the thin layer of clothing he left out in. I'll be back in no time; he had convinced himself before leaving home.

'Got damn Blair, what's taking you so long?" Tom shouted into the darkness.

"Yes? This is Blair."

"Blair, it's Tom."

"Tom, why aren't you here yet? I'm ready to leave."

"Well, that's the issue. I can't make it. My car broke down on the way. I've been standing here in pitch black, stranded with only a flashlight. I'll call Veronica to pick me up, leaving you to sign the papers for mom's release."

"It's no problem, Tom. I just wish I had known that you weren't going to make it here two hours ago."

"Blair, it's not like I planned this. I tried to make it. I am freezing, stuck in the middle of nowhere, like a bald polar bear. Just sign and go."

"Bye!" exclaimed Blair. She hung up in such a frustrating manner all Tom could do was look at his phone in aww.

"She had the nerve to hang up in my face," Tom said, still stunned. Well, let me see if I can get my ass out of here. I pray Veronica picks up her phone, otherwise I will have to sleep in the car, which will lead to an endless night."

Tom dialed Veronica's phone, and to no surprise, she didn't pick up. He hesitantly contacted someone he should have never considered relying on. Ringing upon ringing of the phone went on before he hung up, but as soon as he pulled the phone from his ear, a sexy voice responded to his distress.

"Hey Francine, did my wife drop off Shantell yet? I can't seem to get a hold of her and it's kind of an emergency".

"Well, all the girls played themselves into a coma. Is there anything I can do to help?"

"I am not fond of asking, but I'm stranded on the service street about ten miles from our end of town. I swear I wouldn't ask if I had another choice."

"Not at all, Tom. Helping is not a problem, and my mother can watch the kids until I return. Alternatively, I can swing by your house and deliver the message to your wife," said Francine with a chuckle.

"Ha, ha hilarious. That's the last thing I want. I don't even want her to know I have your number or that I called you to come and rescue me."

"Just to let you know Tom, I was just joking with you. I wouldn't cause any more problems for you than you already may be dealing with. Insinuating much more than just obvious. Tom, no worries. Do you know where you are now? "Somewhere that may sound familiar to me."

"I'm uncertain if you're acquainted with the area, but it lies on the street to the left, facing the old strip mall undergoing renovations to become a bank on Brayden parkway."

"Yes," said Francine. I know exactly the location you're referring to. I was a regular shopper there."

"Travel along that street for approximately five miles. My car will be on the right side. I will put on my hazard lights so you can see me. Francine, be careful. This road lacks streetlights.

"Got it Tom, give me about thirty minutes and I should be there.

"Thanks Francine, I can't thank you enough. See you soon," said Tom.

As much as Tom needed help, Francine wouldn't dare to mess up the opportunity to make sure she prepared herself by freshening her look and reapplying perfume. Before leaving, she peeked in on the girls and informed her mom. The start of Francine's car woke Dabria, who was just asleep. She raised her head, checking for other awake girls. Dabria quietly explored mischievous activities before glancing out the window to see Francine leaving the driveway. The house was completely dark, except for a sliver of light entering through the cracks in Francine's mother's room. Dabria's cat-like stealth made this inconsequential. But soon, someone will remind her of the rule of quid pro quo, which she had forgotten on the quest to become reincarnated in human form. Pursuing vengeance centuries ago, she had already paid the price for dabbling in dark magic, which always demands sacrifice. Dabria continued to move around throughout the house until she found Francine's room and took it upon herself to rummage through her belongings collecting a few trinkets along the way the one thing she didn't foresee is being caught by one of Melanie's friends catching her pillaging through things that didn't belong to her in the dark of night. The girl paused, questioning Dabria's presence.

"What are you doing in Miss Sanchez's room?" asked Amber.

"If you must know, I had a nightmare," replied Dabria cunningly.

"I saw you put some of Miss. Sanchez's things into your pocket. "Why did you," asked Amber?

"Amber, I needed a few treasures so that we could play a pirate game.

"I know, but I'm not sure if the others would find it fun."

"Would you play one quick game downstairs before I have everyone else join tomorrow?" asked Dabria.

"No, not really, this doesn't feel ok. Just walking around this dark house. Let's just play in the morning. This this way you can explain it to everyone at the same time." Anyway, I need my inhaler and I think I left it downstairs."

"I saw it when I went to the kitchen a minute ago. In fact, I was going to bring it to you. I saw you using it earlier. How does it help you?" asked Dabria.

"My inhaler helps me breathe better. It's for my lungs," explained Amber.

"It's in my back pocket now. I'll only give it to you if you promise not to tell anyone about the treasures I collected for tomorrow's game, Dabria said, nervously.

"Come on, I need my medicine to stop playing

Amber said as she began wheezing for air. Look, I promise I won't say anything, Shantell. I promise, now give me my medicine. Dabria threw Amber's inhaler, hitting the wall and falling onto the floor, landing at Amber's feet.

"You know Shantell you're not a nice person and I don't think I want to play the game with you tomorrow and neither should anyone else, in fact after I tell everyone what you have done the others won't play with you ever again, Melanie's mom may even take you home while we continue to have fun all weekend," said Amber

"Filled with rage, Dabria wordlessly returned to the room, lying in a fetal position and staring at Amber as she went to bed. Only thirty minutes later Dabria looked up at Amber who had her sleeping bag set up right next to her sister, listening to everyone in the room different sound pitch of snoring surrounded the room except for Amber who still had a wheezing sound but not as distinct as before she used her inhaler. The threats Amber made and the unexpected sight in Francine's room kept occupying Dabria's thoughts.

"I have to put an end to her," Dabria whispered to herself.

Thinking it would be a simple task. Dabria started a murmuring chant "Hii iwe pumzi yako ya mwisho na kusababisha kifo cha papo hapo." Translation, let this be your last breath resulting in instant death, over and over she chanted (hii iwe pumzi yako ya mwisho na kusababisha kifo cha papo hapo) her eyes bleed with intense concentration she repeated her chanting but, nothing happened her confusion at this point had to be put aside to be figured out later right now her being ratted out was only a few hours away, five hours before dawn. For Dabria to improvise, a murderous act surged through that ten-year-old body embodied over a century old soul. Dabria grabbed her pillow and inched towards Amber, raising it over her head and plunging it into Amber's face.

Smothering her wasn't difficult, Dabria outweighed her by at least fifteen pounds and executed her tactic with precision. She straddled Amber with her knees restraining her arms and pressed her chest and hands down on the pillow, leaving no room for her to breathe. Amber movements of struggle ceased almost instantaneously. Dabria seized Amber's inhaler and vigorously rattled it, searching for any remaining medication. Dabria checked the vial and found it half empty. To cover her bases, she pumped out the remaining medication into the air. Then, she placed the inhaler into Amber's lifeless hands, slid back into her sleeping bag to await the outcome of her plan, which would unfold in just a few hours.

CHAPTER 12

We shouldn't

Blinding headlights pulled alongside Tom's stranded car where he had fallen asleep awaiting the arrival of Francine, a few taps on his windshield startled him as he awoke and forgot where he was. A stern voice of authority demanded that he roll down his window. Tom covered his eyes as a flashlight pointed into his eyes, blinded him.

"Hello officer, slurred Tom as he tried to gather his thoughts into complete sentences, Sorry Sir.

The officer quietly tested Tom's awareness by asking for his name. 'Sorry officer, for my hesitation. It's Tom. My name is Tom," he said nervously.

"Do you have a last name?" The officer inquired.
Tom Mason officer," answered Tom.

"Mr. Mason, may I ask why you're parked alongside this road after 1 am asleep? Have you been drinking?"

"No sir," Tom said. I'm having car trouble, and I was waiting for a ride."

"Well, how long ago did you contact anyone for a ride?"

"I'm not completely sure. I think about an hour ago, I sort of dozed off."

"Do you mind handing me your license and registration and stepping out of the car?"

"Sure, no problem. Where do you need me to stand?"

"Stand in front of my vehicle while I run your information."

"May I ask why you need to run my license?"

"As part of our standard procedure, we run someone's license when we suspect them of being intoxicated."

"But I just told you I'm waiting for a ride because I'm having car trouble."

"Mr. Mason, I'll make sure you're not drunk in case you need a ride. Stay put, I'll be back."

"Ok Mr. Mason, all your information is checked out. Do you mind confirming your sobriety by taking a quick test?"

"No, not at all. What do you want me to do?"

"Use your eyes to track my flashlight, no head movement, just right to left. Next, I want you to do as I do. I want you to extend both your arms outward like this and, using your index finger and touch the tip of your nose, rotating each arm back and forth, go ahead."

Tom exhaled on a single breath he had taken at the start of the second test. His frustration was building until interrupted by an approaching car that pulled alongside them and rolled down the window and, luckily, it was a familiar voice.

"What's the problem, officer?"

Francine arrived just in time to support Tom's story to the police.

"And who are you," asked the officer?

"I'm his driver. He called me because his car was giving him issues."

Tom looked at the officer and shook his head. "You see, just as I have previously mentioned, before you made me take those ridiculous tests."

"Mr. Mason, whether you like it or not, I have a job to do, as do you, I assume. You are now free to go. Here's a bit of information for you at no charge. Move your vehicle within two days or I'll return to issue a ticket. In addition, if it's still here in 7 days, I will call the tow truck just as fast as you opened your mouth with those extra remarks used when your ride pulled up," The cop said with malicious intent. Tom's attitude changed; his voice became monotoned as he ended his back-and-forth word exchange with the officer. Tom had to become humble before he embarrassed himself in front of Francine and ended up in cuffs.

"Come on Tom," exclaimed Francine let's get you home.

After Tom sat inside the car, he thanked Veronica for coming, but not before rolling down the window to antagonize the officer one last time. Tom waved at him with a huge smile and an arrogant smile as he and Veronica drove off.

"Wow Tom, you're a terrible boy I see," said Francine.

In a low sexy voice, entangled with mild seductive actions only seconds into entering her car. Tom couldn't lie to himself between what seemed like flirtatious actions from Francine and her body, putting out such an alluring smell of what smells like a of mix vanilla and perhaps lavender perfume. Giving it the ole college trying to deter the conversation towards a more appropriate one.

"No, not at all Francine, I'm just glad you came. I would have called you to make sure you were on the correct path to meet me, but my phone died."

"That would explain your phone going to voicemail. I tried calling you also at least three times to make sure you still needed me. I didn't want you getting impatient and calling your wife instead."

"Not at all, I guess I could have called her but explaining directions to her is like trying to show someone with dyslexia how to read, just difficult as hell and I don't have many friends I can count on."

"Lucky me," said Francine. Looks like I'm the winner, they both laughed enjoying each other.

"Oh wow, you drive fast Francine," said Tom. Sounding a little disappointed that the ride ended in no time. No, it seems like such, but when you're enjoying yourself, time flies by when you don't want it to end."

"Where should I drop you off? Dare I push the envelope and drop you in front of your house or stay here on the corner"

"Well for one I'm not walking to my house in this dangerous neighborhood," Tom said jokingly. Besides I doubt Veronica is up at 3 am, so the answer to your question is to drop me in front of my house."

"So, Tom, tell me if I'm imagining things, but are you attracted to me," Francine asked confidently.

"Has it been that obvious," asked Tom?

"I had to ask to be certain.

"Yes, but I'm married, I haven't been happily married for a while. I thought adopting Shantell would be the key to fixing a void that we had in our marriage, but it seems to be pulling us further apart. Now don't mistake what I'm saying as regret for adopting Shantell. We adore her, but our parenting skills and ideas for Shantell differ."

"Have you ever asked Shantell what's best for her? She seems intelligent enough to express her feelings about the decisions you two may not agree on, explained Francine. You know Tom, I was going to try kissing you tonight, but in the light of this conversation, I may take a rain check.

"I understand what you're saying, well, how about a hug," asked Francine?

"That I can do."

Embracing across the car console, they relished the

moment, cherishing each other's scent to hold onto it after parting. Releasing their embrace, Tom said thank you one last time before unlatching the door to leave, but Francine grabbed his arm and pulled him into a kiss. As quickly as it happened, it was over. Francine shied away.

"I'm sorry Tom." I just been wanting to give it a shot and who knows, it could have been my last chance."

Tom gazed at her, assuring her not to apologize as he wasn't sorry either. This time, he kissed her, then left the car and quietly entered the house. Francine sat there for a second, touching her lips, being sent to a magical space before snapping back to reality and driving away.

CHAPTER 13

When my eyes are closed, I still see you.

Francine made it back home and turned into her driveway. Dabria watched as the light shined through the window. Curious about Francine's late departure. Abandoning them at the house with an old lady that can barely feed herself, let alone watch a group of young girls. Despite the dead body nearby, Dabria simply feigned sleep. Francine checked on the girls before bed, ensuring breakfast plans and the day ahead. Dozing off, she swiftly drifted into memories of the kiss she shared with Tom.

There were three hours left to rest, which felt like

only seconds before the alarm abruptly rang, jolting her awake to a house filled with screaming girls who had beaten her to the punch. They were already making a mess of the kitchen as they prepared their own breakfast, comprising several things. She understood the day would be lengthy and draining. Francine looked around, noticing that she was one member short.

"Carla, where's your sister?" asked Francine. All the girls answered except Dabria.

She was still asleep they shouted. "Well, can one of you girls wake her for breakfast," asked Francine. She wondered how someone could sleep through all the turmoil that consumed the house.

"I'll do it," answered Dabria, hoping to get ahead of the initial reaction that should take place. She saw her killings as an art form, striving for perfection.

"Thank you, Shantell, you girls hurry back so y'all can finish eating. I planned a day at the water park for you all. Yea! the girls screamed with excitement."

Reaching the room, Dabria double-checked to ensure her malicious act had been flawlessly executed. Dabria prepared her face from a relaxed one to a sad and confused one before entering back into the kitchen.

"Miss. Sanchez Amber doesn't want to get up."

"What do you mean Shantell? Did you shake her?"

"Yes, Ms. Sanchez." answered Dabria.

Francine ran to the room shouting. "Amber wake up honey, wake up."

Francine kneeled beside Amber, inching closer with a worried look, thinking the worst. She aggressively shook her, then rested her head against the chest of Amber's corpse. Bursting into tears confirming what she already knew that Amber was dead. Dabria prepared for a scream but, to her dismay, none came. In walked Carla, asking about her sister. Pancakes muffled her words, making them perplexing.

"Miss. Sanchez, did Amber get up yet? When we're at home, she's always playing the game possum, but I know the secret to getting her up. You have to tickle her belly."

Carla walked towards Amber's body. Francine stopped to gather herself. Francine tilted her head and wiped her eyes so that Carla wouldn't notice her tears.

"Carla don't worry, I'll wake her in my secret way. Please return to the kitchen and finish eating. Instruct others to refrain from entering until I give permission."

Carly walked back to the kitchen, wearing a confused and unsuspecting expression. Her lack of understanding for the room's off-limits status saddened her due to her sister's silence. Francine yelled out, mom, can you please bring the phone to me in Melanie's room? With phone and cane in hand, Francine's mother entered the room, frail and determined.

"Here you go, Francine," said her mom.

Francine sobbed as she grabbed the phone from her mother's hand.

"What's wrong?" asked her mom,

"Carla, she's dead."

The fragile old lady looked down at Amber and stumbled backwards onto the floor. Francine dashed to her mother and sat her mother on the bed and checked to see if her mother had injured herself and dialed 911.

"Yes hello 911 have an emergency. There's a little girl. here she's. I think she's dead. She's not breathing. I don't know what happened and my mother may need some medical attention as well. No, it's not my daughter, it's my daughter's friend. Just, just get here stuttering with nervousness. Please! Yes, my address is 974 Sycamore Lane, yes Sycamore, please hurry."

Francine could hear the girls in the front of the house asking questions to Carla, wondering if something was wrong. In her panic, she nearly forgot to call Amber and Carla's parents.

"What will you tell the girls?" asked Francine's mother in her weakened state?

"I don't know," said Francine. I really don't know." She sat beside her mother, staring at Amber's body.

Cars started showing up at Francine's house before the ambulance even arrived, filled with frantic parents barging their way into her house. In fear of accidents, she withheld information from the parents as they traveled. She urgently notified them about a situation with the kids, requiring their immediate arrival. None of the parents imagined an injured arm or leg perhaps, although still injuries of concern it was still better than the news they were about to receive. The clueless parents shouted for their kids in unison, as if they had planned it. Breanna yelled; her mother ran to her checking parts of her daughter's body.

"Are you ok?" her mother asked.

"Yes, mom, why?" The situation caught everyone, including the other girls, off guard. Except Dabria, who was the transgressor. Shantell yelled out.

Dabria stood there insouciantly positioning herself for Mason's embrace.

"Honey, are you ok? Are you hurt?" asked Tom.

"No, I'm ok," she said. Dabria pondered if she wanted to cause more panic amid the situation, she had already created but chose not to enjoy reveling in her performance.

"Carla! Amber! Here mom, Carla, cried out. Are you girls, ok? Yea mom, but Amber's is still asleep." Her mother's blood felt frigid. She knew something was wrong when everyone responded except Amber.

"Sleeping?" Whispering to herself, she noticed Francine in the hallway crying, soon after paramedics swiftly entered through the door behind her. Amber? Amber baby, answer me. Unresponsive, she started running towards the room. Francine threw herself in her path, clutching her. Amber's mother cried out loud. "Let me go! Amber," she shouted. Feeling emotionally distraught as a mother, Francine felt responsible for Amber's death because she had the girls' care entrusted to her.

"She's dead Karen, Amber's dead," said Francine. With remorse in her voice.

Amber's mom broke free from Francine's arms and made it to the room, forcing herself past the paramedics, only to be grabbed again by one of the treatment technicians. What happened to my daughter!"

"Sorry, Ms. We're not sure what happened to your daughter. An autopsy is necessary, but it appears she suffered an asthma attack. We noticed her inhaler on the side. Unfortunately, it was empty."

"Empty!" she exclaimed. "Why it would be empty? I make sure her inhaler is full everyday you hear me, every damn day."

To corroborate his hypothesis, the medical technician gave the inhaler to Amber's mother. Her face showed such a puzzling look.

"Now this is impossible, I know I checked her medicine. I packed it myself, so you mean it's my fault. My daughter's death could be my fault?"

"Mom, what's wrong?" Carla screamed from the front of the house; she wasn't permitted to see her sister in that state. "Mom, what's going on? Amber!" Carla continued to yell.

Something was wrong, she thought to herself. The obvious clues were her sister's confinement, the ambulance, and her mother's tears. Police arrived with an ambulance and were informed by EMTs. They started clearing the area outside the house. Concerned neighbors gathered around. Detectives cleared Francine's home of unrelated individuals after gathering statements from each girl. Among the dwindling chaos, everyone heard a familiar voice in the background.

"Mr. and Mrs. Mason? What are you doing here?" asked Detective Chase.

"Hi detective," said Veronica.

"Hello, Mrs. Mason, why are you guys here?" asked detective Chase.

"Shantell was at the sleepover," answered Veronica.

"An unfortunate situation," said detective Chase."

"Yes, it is," answered Tom.

"Excuse us detective, we have to be going now. Shantell has been through a lot, unless you have questions for us as well."

"No, not now. But I find it strange that wherever there's a body, you guys are involved. Tom walked towards detective Chase. "I don't like what you're insinuating, detective, and if you don't watch it, you'll find yourself in an unpleasant situation."

CHAPTER 14

How did you get this?

As they entered their home, Tom and Veronica couldn't help but ponder Shantell's emotional state and the unsettling news that Amber's mom received, which contrasted with the pain they had endured. This internal conflict brought about a sense of guilt for experiencing such conflicting emotions.

"Shantell, how are you holding up?"

"I'm fine, can I have a snack?" asked Dabria,

"Sure, go ahead." Veronica looked at Tom, perplexed. "Tom, I'm worried Shantell doesn't seem bothered by what happened at all. It seems absurd to me. Is it possible she's indifferent towards certain aspects."

"We're unaware of her past or emotional processing. Set up a meeting with Dr. Whittman to help Shantell deal with her emotions and whatever else she's been hiding."

To secretly listen, Dabria fabricated a snack excuse and hid in the room's corner. Which allowed the Masons to feel they could speak without restriction. Curious to what their thoughts were concerning what happened at the sleepover. Dabria didn't plan to hear that they were seeing Dr. Whittman. Having Dr. Whittman ask her questions snooping around inside her head was nothing for her to handle. Dabria only knew what happened in Shantell's life in brief spurts. Being suppressed within Shantell, she couldn't see all aspects of Shantell's life.

"Damn!" exclaimed Dabria. Remembering that she also couldn't perform any of her voodoo magic to kill Amber "quid pro quo" she said to herself. "That's it I forgot."

Like before, she surrendered her mortality and soul for revenge, a consequence of the long-ago village massacre. Her power vanished as she became human once more. This deal is her weakness. She achieved her desire, but now it's harder without her reality-bending ability.

"Shantell," Veronica shouted?

"Yes, mom." answered Dabria.

"Shantell, your dad and I decided that it's best if you miss school tomorrow."

"What do you mean you and dad decided without

asking me? screamed Dabria. Figuring a tantrum would get her free from seeing Dr. Whittman.

"Excuse me, young lady," said Tom. Intervening with a stern voice. "Who do you think you are? addressing us in such a manner? I understand you went through a lot, especially last night. But I will not stand disrespect from a child. We, as your parents, have decided with no exceptions."

"Parents," asked Dabria. With short bursts of laughter. "You aren't my parents. You saw a black girl and thought adopting me would fix your failing marriage." Tom and Veronica stood in disbelief. Shantell's words shocked them. "Listen here."

"No! hollered Dabria. I'm not going!"

Were her final words before running upstairs to her room hoping that the stunt she had just displayed worked because the reality of it was, she didn't have a choice she was now powerless depending now on her wit and five hundred years of lifetime experiences.

"Leave her alone for tonight, Tom." said Veronica. We'll address it in the morning, I'm drained, I just want to go to bed. Do you think you can run me a bath please, while I go put this load of laundry to wash?"

"Sure, no problem," replied Tom. "But I'll take mine first since you have a few things to do. I'll be quick."

Veronica entered the laundry room and exhaled at the sight of the overwhelming pile of clothes. "Wow, I have to remember it's not only Tom and me now. Well, I have to begin somewhere because the clothes won't wash themselves." Veronica routinely checked clothing pockets before starting the washer, to prevent damage to the machine. While doing so, she discovered Jalicia's charm bangle. "What the hell? Tom!" Yelled Veronica in a jealous rage. Veronica made her way to their bedroom. She banged on the bathroom door furiously. Tom opened the door, perplexed by her frantic knocking.

"What now?" asked Tom.

"What is this, Tom? Because it sure doesn't belong to me," exclaimed Veronica.

Tom recalled the night he and Francine kissed. but that was from nervous guilt. Prior to Francine's arrival, he found the bracelet on the back floor of Veronica's car.

"Why are you asking me? I found it in your car last night while searching for a flashlight to inspect under hood after your car left me stranded."

"It's not mine," Veronica stated. My heart dropped when I pulled it from your pockets. You're cheating, I know it," shouted Veronica.

Tom grabbed her by the arms and pulled her closer to him in a ploy to change the subject. "Honey, I told you I wanted to work on our marriage, although things have been tough. I would never go outside of our marriage. I've never considered cheating on you. Our family is my priority. You, Shantell, and I are my concern. I have no time for anyone else.

"Veronica gave Tom a tight hug. Her love for him is evident in her eyes; she forgot to ask how Tom made it home, she was simply happy he did.

Did you identify the bracelet's owner?" asked Tom.

"Not yet," said Veronica. But I won't worry about it

tonight. We have to focus on urgent matters tomorrow, so I can't consider it now.

"Well, ok," said Tom. I'll run your bath, and then go to sleep.

Veronica put the bracelet onto her dresser drawer to gather her clothes for a soothing hot bath, where she would remain to gather her thoughts. After locking the bathroom door behind her, Veronica removed her clothing. Veronica carefully dipped her toes into the water, recognizing the steam in the air as a sign of its scalding temperature. Veronica slowly submerged her entire body into the water. She laid her head back onto the wall above the tub and placed her steaming hot towel over her eyes and dozed off. Awakened with a disturbing thought, did Shantell steal Jalicia's bracelet? Dr. Whittman expressed how her sister never took off the bracelet. But seeing as someone whom she owns jewelry that she holds sacred, the term never is more rhetorical. Eventually, these things must be removed. "Is Shantell a thief?" she asked herself. Additionally, she must confront Dr. Whittman regarding her daughter's silence and the mystery surrounding the bracelet.

CHAPTER 15

Truth be told

Awakening from a restless night, Veronica turned over to shake Tom from his sleep, which the many attempts proved he hadn't lost a wink and slept straight through like a baby.

"Tom, it's time to wake up. Tom!"

She shook and called his name over and over with a fatigued voice. What? In a cranky tone, Tom asked, which is typical when someone is abruptly awakened from a deep sleep.

"I need you to miss work today," said Veronica.

"For what? Shantell, you understand the situation

from yesterday and I believe I know the owner of the bracelet."

"Who?"

"I believe it belongs to Dr. Whitman's sister.

"The dead one?"

"Yes," she said nervously."

"Why would it be in your car?"

"Tom, I believe Shantell stole it. Oh my god, what's next," asked Veronica?

"Do you know how this looks? It's one thing after another, my mom, Dr. Whittman's sister, not to mention the little girl dying last night," said Tom.

"Listen, don't panic just yet. I must have faith in a positive outcome, after consulting with Dr. Whittman. I think she will understand."

"Ok, wake up. Shantell and I will contact my office and let them know I won't be showing up today, and afterwards I will see if Dr. Whittman can see us today."

Veronica walked to Shantell's room and taped on her door. "Shantell, Shantell honey, it's time to get up, Shantell? but there was no response. Veronica entered the room expecting Shantell's presence, only to find her absent after their heated conversation last night.

"Tom!" yelled Veronica, is Shantell downstairs?"

"Yes, she's in the kitchen eating breakfast and already dressed. Looks like she reconsidered going to see Dr. Whittman." With empathy, Tom put himself in a ten-year-old girl's shoes, considering her tough experiences. "Are you ok with seeing the Doctor today or are my assumptions premature or am I getting ahead of myself?" asked Tom. Placing his arm on her shoulder, symbolizing that he loves her.

"Yes, I'm ok with it," said Dabria, as she filled her mouth with cereal.

With an ulterior motive behind those empty reassurances she was displaying for the Masons, Dabria spent the night pondering on a plan to deceive Dr. Whittman. She couldn't take the chance of being implicated in being anyone but Shantell. No more multiple personality disorders as referred to by previous doctors. Dabria was here to stay. Shantell may be gone, but her persona must remain. Veronica made her way downstairs after getting prepared to leave.

"Tom, what time is the appointment?" asked Veronica. It's really at ten thirty, so that gives us about two hours.

"Yes," yelled Tom.

"Perfect, well hello young lady. How did you sleep last night?" asked Veronica.

"Not great," said Dabria. Going into Shantell mode with apologies from her actions last night. The way I acted was not fair to you guys at all. I just reacted badly because of Amber; I can only imagine how her mom is feeling." Playing Shantell's role almost effortlessly but she knew it wasn't perfect so she couldn't get complacent and remain vigilant. "Hey mom and dad, I was wondering if we could go visit Amber's mom and sister after visiting Dr. Whittman." Tom and Veronica exchanged joyful glances, quietly hopeful.

"Sure, honey," responded Veronica. I'm sure they'll be grateful for the support, but I'll call ahead. We don't want to just show up unannounced. Ladies, we must leave now. Hopefully, traffic won't be an issue."

CHAPTER 16

Can't I or Can I

Stepping into Dr. Whittman's office created a somber atmosphere, as if the once inviting space had been devoid of its warm hues.

"Hello, we're the Masons. We have a ten thirty appointment. You must be the new receptionist," Veronica asked.

"Hello Mr. and Mrs. Mason, yes, I have you guys written in right here, but I'm merely a temporary fill in, until the doctor decides what she wants to do regarding permanently filling the position. I feel she is not quite ready to move on yet."

"Oh my," Gasped Veronica. If you don't mind me asking your opinion how she is mentally?"

"Well, I'm no expert but if you're concerned about her being in the right state of mind to tend to you guys professionally let me just say that I don't believe she would treat any patients if she wasn't ready to do so don't get me wrong, she is still grieving. I mean it was her sister she lost, and she still have unanswered questions."

I appreciate the reassurance," said Veronica.

"No problem, Dr. Whittman, just stepped out for a few minutes. She will be back in a moment. Kindly have a seat in the waiting area."

Dr. Whittman walked in, her elated look welcoming Veronica and Tom with handshakes and Dabria with a hug. "How are you guys doing today? Given its urgency, things are likely in disarray. I made time for you by moving my appointments around."

"Certainly, and please accept my apologies on behalf of all of us for any inconvenience caused."

"Oh god no, not at all. I was happy too. I planned to call you myself if I didn't hear from you soon regarding any issues with the detective visiting Shantell."

"Everything went well that day. Everything that followed took a turn for the worse."

"Hopefully, I can be of some help today. Follow me into my office. Let's begin by sharing what has been concerning all of you. Who wants to go first?"

"I will," said Dabria.

Curiosity filled Tom and Veronica as they observed

her, oblivious to her eagerness to speak. "First, I would like to apologize to my parents." Practiced words, gaining trust and touching soft spots, obvious action of Shantell. "And I would like to say that since I couldn't sleep last night, I wrote a poem explaining my feelings.

"Sounds amazing Shantell," said Dr. Whittman, glancing at Mr. and Mrs. Mason. "Ready to hear her out? It's important to listen before reacting to each other. Dabria dug into her pocket and inhaled, followed by a long exhale.

"Darling it's ok, don't be nervous. Go ahead we're listening, and we won't judge you."

"Ok here I go," said Dabria. "I've been there. Nowhere else matters, only here - with my new parents who chose me. Despite my imperfections and emotional ways, I guess I stood out to you, above all the rest. A chance is what I needed; a life is what you gave me. Who knows, what you guys need to know is you saved me. I will not be the angel which you deserve, but I will try my best to love you as much as you do me described in one word 'Family."

Veronica teared up instantly. Almost not wanting to, she mentioned the bracelet Tom found in her car due to her emotions. She knew it would implicate Shantell as thief, and to them she was just a troubled little girl that needed a chance to prove herself. To fix their issues and start positively, everything had to be addressed now. Besides, it wouldn't be fair to Dr. Whittman, who needed closure. Perhaps having her sister's charm bracelet back would provide some closure.

"I think it's time to show her the bracelet." Veronica whispered into Tom's ear. Tom nodded in agreement.

"Dr. Whittman, I have something to show you. I hope you understand that we found this and hid it to protect what we love."

"In this place, we don't judge you for your feelings, just be honest."

Veronica reached into her purse and pulled out the bracelet. Dabrias' eyes remained fixated on the bracelet in disbelief. Despite her wrongdoings, the bracelet was forgotten about once more. Despite her attempt to resolve the situation with the Masons through a letter, she once again ended up on the defensive. Dr. Whittman's heart dropped.

"My God! Where did you find it?"

"Well, Tom found it in the back floor of my car," said Veronica.

"Listen Doctor, Veronica and I have concluded that Shantell may have picked it up by mistake.

"The detectives asked her about this bracelet, and she all out lied about it." Dr. Whittman exclaimed emotionally.

"Dr. Whittman, we acknowledge the wrongdoing, and she now recognizes the error. As you know, she's been through a lot and she's only ten," explained Veronica as she wept.

"I suppose you're right and as a professional, it's my job to get to the core of the issues and not act on emotions. May I briefly speak with Shantell alone, even though there's additional matters to discuss with both of you? From what I gather, she is the main reason you guys had to get in to speak to me today."

"Yes, it is."

The Masons apologized to Dabria for their actions, which worsened the situation. Dabria stared at the door until the Masons exited the room, then she focused on her words carefully. Cunning as the doctor may be at getting people to expose themselves, had nothing on her centuries of deception made her even more cunning than Dr. Whittman. But the doctor wasn't on a quest to know what Shantell's heart needed to move forward but to dig deeper into why she had her sister's bracelet, in her mind if she lied about the bracelet, she may have concealed vital information concerning your sister's death perhaps she saw more than she led everyone to believe.

"Shantell, tell me what's been going on recently. Can you tell me why your parents are so concerned about your behavior?" asked Dr. Whittman.

Dabria took a minute to figure out where Dr. Whittman may head with her questions before replying. Dabria subtly shifted the conversation's focus, keeping her true motives hidden from the doctor.

"I don't know," said Dabria. Perhaps I've been having a hard time because my parents have been arguing a lot lately and they don't know that I can hear how often they fuss, and it sounds like most of it has been about me. I think they regret adopting me."

"Shantell, that's not the case. Your parents have told

me on occasions that adopting you was the best decision they ever made."

"Doctor, I don't understand why my mother would tell me hide the bracelet but share it with you. I know taking it wasn't the right choice. I wanted to return it after she saw me, but she made me promise to keep it a secret.

"Shantell, why would your mother deny saying or making you do that?"

"Maybe she just thought I would get in a lot of trouble," said Dabria shrewdly as she continued her elaborate story. Mom has been acting strangely, throwing things and fussing with the teachers at my school. Now some kids tease me because of it.

Dr. Whittman sat there leery of Shantell's accusations but couldn't disregard them either. "Shantell, I want to ask you one more question before we're done with our session. Just know whatever you tell me about this question won't be told to your parents. It will be our secret."

"Ok" replied Dabria, emulating the look of fear as she responded, making sure the doctor knew how scared she was, or wanted her to believe.

"Shantell the day that you picked up the bracelet, choosing her words wisely the doctor didn't want to use words like stole, or took so she can continue trusting her not to make Shantell feel as it maybe her fault and not tell her the answers she needed. "Did you see anyone else here in the office area where you were," asked the doctor.

Dabria quickly answered the question without hesitation. She had already fabricated a story that should fit perfectly. "Mommy briefly checked on me while Ms. Jalicia was in the bathroom. She left, instructing us to stay as our time here was limited. After using the bathroom, she returned and went into your office." Dabria had masterminded such a conniving story that she herself had believed it. Those five minutes that Veronica went to check on Shantell combined with Dr. Whittman's need for closure was enough to spark an investigation towards veronica. Despite the five-minute round trip to the office, the murder of her sister didn't account for enough time. Yet, it was sufficient for the doctor's probable cause.

"Shantell, this is the end of our session. Remember, hush hush on what you told me about what we spoke of it our secret. Now let's go see how your mom and dad are doing."

Veronica and Tom immediately stood up when the doorknob of Dr. Whittman's office started turning in anticipation of how things went, wondering if the doctor could make some progress in having Shantell open more.

"How did it go." asked Veronica.

"Honestly, she and I made a little progress. As you know, Veronica, these things take time and Shantell's case is delicate. I would have to request her files from her prior therapist so I can see where things started. Another doctor's documentation will make things much easier to assess," explained Dr. Whittman.

"We understand, did Shantell mention what happened to the little girl," asked Tom.

"No, she didn't, what happened?" asked Dr. Whittman.

"Shantell attended a sleepover where a young girl passed away in her sleep. Although the girls were present, they were oblivious to her death. Apparently, they just figured she was still asleep, but we explained everything to Shantell the best way we could, she didn't seem to be phased by it." explained Veronica.

"Well Mrs. Mason, I can only assume two things and I hate assuming without properly getting to the core. As a concerned parent, I think she may be desensitized due to her experiences. Maybe she's still in shock and reality hasn't set in yet. But it's something we can address the next time we meet."

"Thanks, doctor, we appreciate you making time to see us today." said Veronica. Shantell, are you ready? I know you wanted to go check on Amber's mom. I phoned her while you were with Dr. Whittman, and she said we could stop by. Carla needs all the support she can get. It's clear that losing her sister is having a significant impact on her. In fact, if you don't mind and they're willing, I would like to refer them to you, Dr Whittman. Maybe you can help them in their time of grieving."

"Sure, I will help if I can. The busier the better. It helps me keep my mind off my sister and thank you so much for returning my sister's. bracelet. It's all I have left of her now."

"No need for thanks. Anyway, someone shouldn't have taken it, and I'm glad you understand the conditions in which Shantell picked it up."

"Yes, Shantell, Dr. Whittman repeated insistently to gauge Veronica's reaction, but there was no sign. Suggesting that Veronica was completely unaware of the details she had just received from Shantell and assumed she was successfully evading blame for the crime.

"Ok doctor, until next time," said Tom, waving goodbye before Dr. Whittman called him back.

"Tom, do you have a second?" asked Dr. Whittman.

"Sure," said Tom. Honey, why don't you pull the car around? I will be there in a minute.

Veronica looked back multiple times, perplexed by the Doctor's exclusive interest in Tom. Perhaps she wants to know if I have been keeping up with my own medications and progression, Veronica wondered. Deemed to have been untrustworthy. I can see why she wouldn't take my word for it yet.

"Is something wrong?" asked Tom.

With a hint of concern, he himself was wondering why she called him back. "Hey Tom, I won't keep you. I had a question about your wife that I didn't want to ask in front of her. Shantell mentioned something that I find concerning and it may be connected to her past diagnosis."

"Okay," said Tom, Baffled by the statement. What concern could Shantell have mentioned that he didn't know about? Tom thought.

"To be straightforward," said the doctor, "I don't

know how to ask." Tom Shantell mentioned anything to you about Veronica having her lie or keeping secrets about things."

Things? Similar situations occurred, including Shantell's disclosure of Veronica's awareness of the missing bracelet and her plea for secrecy. "What!" exclaimed Tom Shantell said that? If this is indeed the case, doctor, I honestly cannot fathom anything rationale behind her actions, unless she initially believed she was shielding Shantell. However, I am unsure why she would deceive me, especially after discovering it in my laundry and suggesting that I may have been unfaithful. It's just too overwhelming. Losing my mother, the tragic incident involving the little girl, your sister's troubles, the constant interrogation by the detectives, my demanding job, and now this."

"Tom, is Veronica still taking her medications like she should?"

"At first, she wasn't, but I started making sure she did by watching her take them myself. I figured after monitoring her for a while like we agreed everything would be fine, but it seems like she may be skipping them again. Dr. Whittman offered condolences for Tom's mother and chose not to disclose further information in Shantell's session.

"No worries." said Dr. Whittman. In fact, didn't even mention it to Veronica. I promised Shantell I wouldn't say anything. She and I are just beginning to build trust between one another. If there are other possibilities, I recommend thoroughly exploring them.

But I believe she will push back, and we don't want that."

"If you think that's best, I won't say anything," said Tom.

"Please ensure her continued therapy attendance and medication compliance. I also want to see Shantell again as soon as possible. Her change will be challenging, just her and me in sessions, if that's okay."

"Whatever you believe will help," said Tom. Before Veronica questions what's happening, I should leave. I am confident that she is already aware. I will call you next week to make another appointment."

Veronica sat in the car, tapping her fingers, waiting for Tom. Her mind misleading her to be more curious than usual. The heightened curiosity in her mind made her question if this conversation was truly professional. Unable to tolerate it any further, she shifted the gear into the park position. Before opening the door, Veronica notices Tom approaching the car, causing a momentary pause.

"Sorry I took so long ladies. Are you ready to head home?"

"I thought we were going to Amber's house. Don't you guys still want to see how they are doing? I want to see Carla and Melanie, they are supposed to be there also," cried Dabria.

She exaggerated her concerns, solely preoccupied with identifying any issues with killing Amber. The kill was clean, no evidence left. She needed certainty.

"Right, I forgot. Let's go. What did Dr. Whittman want?" asked Veronica.

"Nothing much," said Tom. She just wanted some information dealing with rebranding her office with the new advertisement. And if it's something my company can take care of."

"That's great, I assume it will be something you will handle yourself. I mean, you're the one bringing her business to your firm."

With eagerness, Tom declared that it was his plan to enhance the credibility of his lie. Which worked well because the constant questions ceased abruptly.

CHAPTER 17

Condolences

"We made it," said Veronica.

"Are you sure? There's lots of cars," said Tom.

"This is the address she gave me.

"Look, there's Melanie, Dabria shouted.

"Well, I guess that answers that question. I mean, realistically, I know we couldn't have been the only ones that wanted to check one of them. Looks like a crowd, so a combination of family and friends would explain the lack of parking spots. "I'll tell you what," said Tom. "Both of you, get out here and I'll do my best to find a spot. If I can't find a spot nearby, I'll just park at a nearby store and you can call me when you're finished."

"Good idea," said Veronica, "We won't be long.

"Send my condolences to the family please," asked Tom.

"Sure, honey I will," said Veronica. Let's go Shantell."

"Bye dad," said Dabria. "See you soon," dashing into Melanie's arms before the car door could close.

"Hi Melanie," said Dabria.

"Hi, Shantell. Could you tell me why you are here alone?" asked Dabria.

"Carla started crying, and it just made me sad."

"Any other school kids here?" asked Dabria passively. Her caring about Melanie's feelings was nowhere near her thoughts, even with the tears that started moving down Melanie's cheeks.

"Hey Melanie, are you ok? asked Veronica, when she noticed her crying. She approached Melanie with a hug until she stopped crying. "It's going to be alright Mel. I know you all are hurting as you should, but it will be ok. Let's go inside with the others."

Veronica pushed the doorbell, which was almost unnoticeable with all the voices inside, overshadowing the ringing. Ignoring the unanswered doorbell, Veronica and the girls casually entered. Veronica could feel the sorrow as soon as they entered the house. The atmosphere felt damp, probably from the salty tears that embodied the air.

"Kids, go find Carla and make sure she's okay," said Veronica. Noticing Carla and Amber's mother secluded in the corner of her kitchen. Veronica walked over to her as she stared fixatedly at what seemed to be a toy. "Hello

Karen, Karen didn't respond, "Karen? With a touch on her arm, she called out Karen's name once more, hoping for a response. Karen raised her pale face up towards Veronica in a daze. She didn't even flinch when unexpectedly being touched by Veronica. As if she was sitting in an empty house that wasn't being occupied by a multitude of visitors. Hey Karen, momentarily losing track of who Veronica was, being that they only met during a heinous situation." I'm so sorry if I startled you, Shantell, and I finally made it here. Apologies for the delay. We had a prior appointment and weren't certain if you wished to be bothered."

"It's alright Veronica, Carla and I could use the distraction, otherwise I would just be here, closed off from the world. Perhaps even distance myself from Carla. She doesn't deserve that. She's also in pain. They were profoundly close."

"I can't even imagine your feelings. Besides that, I experienced the loss of a child, and it crushed me profoundly. I couldn't handle the idea that my child was no longer with us, explained Veronica."

"I'm sorry to hear that. How did you get past it? Well, I didn't get past it. I just had to get help so I could cope with it. I didn't think I needed it until I started lashing out at people around me that didn't deserve it. The mornings were tough, lacking motivation to get up and just dragging myself around. And my husband, although he was supportive and understood, I wasn't being fair to him by neglecting my duties as a wife. I then agreed to get help from a therapist."

"You mean a psychiatric doctor? "Look, I'm not crazy, just grieving," said Karen, in a defensive manner.

"Needing to speak to someone doesn't make you crazy. Initially, I shared your mindset. Expressing yourself without fear of judgment is liberating. Karen don't worry about deciding now. If you need to talk, I'm here for you. So, here's my therapist card. I mentioned this in case you feel the need to bring Carla."

"Thanks, I will consider it. We will both face a tough transition. I know this may be asking a lot, but Melanie will occasionally have play dates with Carla to divert her attention from fixating on her sister. Do you mind if Shantell joined them also? The more the merrier," said Keren.

Let me know ahead of time and I will ensure Shantell is prepared. Did you hear anything else about Amber's passing?" asked Veronica.

"They called this morning and mentioned her condition worsened due to lack of eosinophil medicine. Further investigation revealed a defective inhaler. I'll get a lawyer to handle my case against the pharmaceutical company this week."

"Wow, sorry again, but at least you have some closure, knowing it wasn't your fault, especially knowing you always check her medications. Is Melanie here with her mother, or was she dropped off?" Veronica asked, hoping to elicit more information from Karen about her daughter's care when she passed away. But she didn't go into depth as Veronica hoped. She just answered the question and gave nothing more.

"Let me introduce you to some of my family and friends."

Running into the girls, Veronica suggested to Karen that they were behaving like a pack of wild animals. "Girls, hey girls," Karen shouted. Can you please play outside?"

"Ok mom," answered Carla.

Before Carla finished answering, Dabria and Melanie were already halfway out the door. "Wait!" yelled Carla. "You guys wait for me," as she trailed behind.

As soon as they put a significant distance between the house and themselves, Dabria wasted no time in immersing herself. Eager to extract information that Carla may possess regarding her sister's corpse.

"So, Carla was Amber's body cold? Did you touch her after she died?" asked Dabria.

"Shantell stopped being weird," said Melanie. Being those things such as death and everything in a scary capacity frightened her.

"It's ok," said Carly. "They didn't allow me to touch her."

"But what do you think she looked like?" asked Dabria, continuing to push the conversation. "Do you think it's like in the movies with the bodies turning color with a gross smell like a zombie?"

"I'm going by the swings. I don't want to hear these things, exclaimed Melanie."

Right after Melanie walked away, Dabria badgered Carla even more, demanding an answer. I guess so," said Carla. I never really thought about it. All I know is that I miss her already.

"Heaven or hell?" asked Dabria.

"What?" asked Carla. Do you think she will go to heaven or hell," Dabria asked, sitting there with anticipation of at least seeing Carla break into tears from her forceful unfiltered questions.

But nothing. Carla just answered the question. "Well, according to my mom, my sister will go to heaven. She said her and my dad are together there and will be happy now. My dad won't be alone anymore and one day we will all be a family again."

"Shantell!" Dabria heard someone yelling in the distance Tom had returned to pick them up.

"Tell your mom I'm back," yelled Tom.

"Is it time to go?" asked Dabria.

"Yes, go tell your mom."

Dabria mentioned to Carla that she must leave but will inquire to her mom about returning.

Melanie walked Dabria her and Carla, feeling relieved. She sensed something unfamiliar and unpleasant from Shantell. The girl that was picked on at the beginning that first walked into her classroom was now saying weird things, giving her eerie vibes. Upon preparing to leave Karen's home, Dabria hugged Carla.

"Carla, everything will be ok I promise, and you will see your sister and dad again, very soon!" Whispered Dabria into Carla's ear.

"Ok young lady, time to go," said Veronica. Dad's waiting.

"Thanks again for coming. We will consider our conversation about Carla and I speaking to a professional."

Tom's frustration heightened, and he started blaring the horn, causing a disruption in traffic flow. Strangely enough, Melanie avoided Dabria when they left. She just stared at her as they drove away the whole time Dabria waved at her with malice.

"Shantell how was Carla holding up?" asked Veronica. I didn't speak to her much but I'm sure she would have spoken to you more openly than she spoke to me.""

"She wasn't speaking much. She seemed sad and was saying some strange things."

"Strange things like what?" asked Veronica with concern.

"Hold on, let me think. She tried stalling for the most outlandish lie she could think of. But nothing too extravagant that may cause immediate attention to be watched every day. "She was saying things like she wished she could be with Amber and her dad right now."

"Sounds like a girl with a broken heart and rightfully so, considering her loss," said Veronica. "She didn't say anything about hurting herself or anyone, I hope." Carla's safety, along with the safety of the other kids, concerned Veronica.

"No, I don't think so."

"I remember Melanie kept interrupting her from saying things. Carla's words failed to capture her interest. Well, that didn't seem very nice. I didn't think Melanie was so unsympathetic. Make sure you don't pick up those habits, your dad and I want you to consider everyone's feelings. Tom agreed with Veronica and added that if someone doesn't treat her with respect, she should let them know.

"Okay, I will." said Dabria. Are we heading home now? I'm so tired.

"Are you hungry? We can pick up something to eat before heading home. I'm sure the snacks I saw you eating over at Carla's house didn't fill you up."

"No, I'm just tired," Dabria said, fatigued.

"Tom, we can stop if you want something to eat, said Veronica.

"I'll find something later at home. She seems tired and we're not too far from home, anyway. We've all had a long day. He muffled his phone as best he could, trying to silence the multitude of calls he was receiving from Francine. "Tom, is that your phone that keeps ringing?" Veronica inquired with interest.

"Yes, there was an issue at work earlier, but I assured them I would take care of it, I let them know I was with my family, handling an emergency. I'll fix it when I get home."

So confidently, that he said he would believe the same tale as a momentary cover-up. Desperate to silence Francine's incessant calls, Tom swiftly headed inside the house and dialed her number from the bathroom. Tom started his bath with the water running slow enough to give him time to return Francine's call to a perfect place to be because the water drowns out any conversations, he may have that he didn't want Veronicas to overhear. Tom took his phone from his pocket and dialed Francine's number.

"Hello," answered a disheartened Francine.

"Francine, why do you keep calling my phone almost nonstop? I'm with my family." Tom heard sobbing sounds with words of desperation to follow.

"Tom, I need you. I'm having a hard time dealing with Amber's death, especially not knowing if it happened while we're together."

"Listen Francine, you need to calm down we will never know what time her death occurred. It could have happened moments after you returned home or hours after. So, you could have been there when it happened but also couldn't have prevented it no matter which way it went."

Tom whispered trying to stay below the sounds of the running water. Tom, how much longer will you stay in there?" Veronica shouted as she knocked on the door. "Shantell wants you to read her a story before going to sleep." Tom covered the phone as he spoke to his wife, leaving Francine paused on the other line.

"I'll be there as soon as I'm done, honey. It shouldn't take me long."

Ok, I'll let her know you will be there soon, said Veronica.

"Look Francine that night I appreciate you coming pick me up when I needed help, but the kiss shouldn't have happened. I admit there has been a lingering itch of attraction on my part and I'm sure it was there for you also, but I need to make sure my family works and when I needed someone to listen to, you were there to do so. But it won't happen again."

Francine's anger flared as she insisted. Tom, this discussion is far from finished," exclaimed Francine.

The phone went silent, followed by the buzzing tone. Tom muttered under his breath, expressing disbelief at Francine's abrupt phone disconnection. After fifteen minutes, Tom opened the bathroom door and was startled by Veronica, who stood nearby.

"Finally, I can use the bathroom and you took longer than normal," said Veronica. I needed my feminine items. Tom suggested she use the downstairs bathroom if it was truly urgent. "Tom, I wasn't making a big deal about it. I was just saying and besides, I figured you wouldn't have taken you so long. If I would have gone downstairs, you would have been coming out." Tom's passive attitude towards Veronica's menstrual cycle surprised her. "I needed things in this bathroom."

Tom forgot that Francine was still on the phone, Francine hung up abruptly, leaving Tom rattled and confused. He acknowledged the peril of a scorned woman. He shook his head and proceeded to Shantell's room. Slowly opening the door, Tom called out, "Shantell, are you awake? I'm here to read you that story you asked for." Firmly tucked in, Dabria answered with a somnolent response.

"I was waiting for your dad, but I guess I fell asleep. Could you read it to me tomorrow?"

"Sure honey, go back to sleep. I'm sorry I took so long, but tomorrow I promise." Tom kissed her on the forehead and readjusted the covers across her chest.

CHAPTER 18

Lust over love

Tom's typical day involved dropping off Shantell at school before going to work. But so many things have happened during the weekend that altered their routine. The passing of Tom's mother, the passing of Amber, and not to mention the ultimate lack of judgment kissing Francine. It's strange how quickly things can go wrong for someone who appears to have everything in order. Dropping Shantell off to school was an awkward one. Francine, although attending to direct other student drop off areas, made her way to Tom before he could pull off.

"Well hello Tom," said Francine. Tom anticipated

a dramatic spectacle after their previous conversation, but found it wasn't so bad.

"Hello Francine, just trying to make it too work. My plate is overflowing with tasks at the moment."

Dabria remained seated in the car, unaffected by Francine's obstruction and lack of urgency. Tom demanded that Francine step aside and allow Shantell to exit the car. Dabria noticed the switch in their normal greetings.

"Go ahead honey it's ok, have a good day at school. Francine, what do you think you're doing? I mean seriously blocking my car door, preventing my daughter from getting out. You should stop. Evident in my prior statement; I love my wife, better yet, I love my family. Understand, you're about to cause a scene.

Francine giggled, "Tom, I didn't know you were so self-centered. I believe you're making more of that meaningless, and might I add a horrible kiss, I had better," exclaimed Francine. She looked for a reaction that she didn't expect by taunting his ego.

"Well, I guess that's it. We have an understanding. Normalcy can be restored from this point. "Sure," said Francine with discernable sarcasm.

However, Tom no longer wanted to continue the discussion. "Bye Miss. Sanchez." Showing that their relationship will now just be a professional one. "Bye Tom!" Yet, a mere professional bond was not what she had in mind. Moments later, not even 15 minutes after the children had settled into their first period class, the intercom came on. Mrs. Clemens can you please send

Shantell Mason to the office please?" The class was familiar with Shantell Mason, although it was unusual for her to be addressed by her complete name.

"Ohm you're in trouble," the class shouted in an uproar. Mrs. Clemens told Shantell that she could be excused. But go straight to the counselor's office to see Miss. Sanchez. "Yes, ma'am," said Dabria. Her curiosity peaked, recalling the awkwardness between Tom and Francine from this morning's drop off. Upon Dabrias' arrival, Miss. Sanchez had the door open and the notorious chair. The chair was where most people sat, and no matter how hard the kids tried, they expressed all their feelings and secrets that they swore to keep amongst themselves. You see, the irony of it all, although she had many issues of her own, some worse than others, she helped with their problems. She should be lying down on someone's couch herself, Dabria thought. But here we go. This should be interesting, Dabria murmured. She thinks she's dealing with Shantell, who had the mental strength of a wet cracker. Ok, let the mind melting games begin.

"Please come in," Miss Sanchez said with a pleasant tone. Have a seat over here.

"Ok Miss. Sanchez," said Dabria.

"I guess you're wondering why I called you in here. Well, I sometimes like to keep in touch with the new kids, but this is special considering Amber's passing this weekend. I will try to fit in sessions for you guys as much as possible to make sure you're coping. I've been speaking to Melanie daily. She's going through a tough time."

"How are you dealing with things," asked Miss Sanchez.

"I'm not sure, I mean no disrespect," said Dabria, but I didn't know her. I don't call meeting someone for a few hours knowing someone.

"Shantell, I expected more sympathy from you. It's strange that Amber's passing doesn't touch you. Dabria was tired of the facade that she was playing for Miss Sanchez.

"Ok Francine let's change the subject," exclaimed Dabria, unmasking the Shantell persona.

"Young lady, who do you think you're speaking to? Do you want me to call your father?"

"I'm sure you would like that," said Dabria.

"Shantell, I don't know what's wrong with you or what you're getting at, but you're way out of line."

"Francine, please don't be coy. I'm not as dumb as you may think. I notice your gaze towards Tom. However, I wasn't certain until this morning's incident when you blocked the door. You made a statement, and it seems you have feelings for him."

Francine sat there, baffled. "Who are you?" asked Francine. I'm going to call your father. You're not the girl I met a few weeks ago."

"You're right, I'm not the same person and if you want to keep your job and save face in front of your peers, then leave me the hell alone. That also includes Veronica and Tom. Francine, I believe this meeting is over, and please for future purposes next time you hold a pajama party, it wouldn't be a good idea to leave kids in the house with someone that needs to be watched herself. I mean come on, your mother. She's sick, herself, I can't stop laughing just thinking about it. I'm surprised she didn't die that night along with Amber," said Dabria. Although it offered little consolation, Amber's inhaler wasn't faulty, I may have helped with that. With a smug expression, Dabria left the office. Releasing her true self, even in a small intervention, felt exhilarating. Francine wondered about the death of Amber after meeting Shantell's host, Dabria. Although she didn't know her identity, the evil within Shantell's body slowly manifested.

...

CHAPTER 19

Viable evidence

After learning about the fabricated information from Dabria, Dr. Whittman called Detective Chase. (Phone rings) and detective Chase picks up.

"Hello?" In a low raspy voice, he answered.

"Hello detective, this is Dr. Whittman. Sounds like you were sleeping. Sorry to wake you."

"Dr. Whittman, do you know what time it is? It's 2 am couldn't whatever you need waited?"

"Not for me detective, I have been struggling all day with whether I should call you or not."

"Couldn't you have struggled a few more hours? I

mean, if it was an emergency, 911 would have been a better choice."

"I couldn't sleep with this on my mind. It's regarding my sister. Today, I met with the Masons and their daughter, Shantell, and shared intriguing thoughts about her mother."

"Ok Doc, go ahead. I'm up now so you might as well tell me what information you have, ideally, it's something we can use."

"Well, I had a one-on-one session with their daughter but not before Mr. Mason told me he found my sister's bracelet in the back seat of his wife's car which ended up in his pocket where Mrs. Mason supposable found it in his pants pocket while doing the laundry."

"Doctor, I'm tired. I assume you will get to the core. You know, Detective, if the death of my sister is cutting into the few hours of sleep you have left, I apologize, but remember you will wake up and my sister won't ever again.

"I'm sorry," said Detective Chase. I tend to be an asshole when I'm tired. Go ahead, I'm listening!

"Look, the Masons came by the office because they said they were having issues with their daughter and ended up telling me that Shantell stole my sister's bracelets, well they didn't use the word stole of course, which wasn't a tremendous deal. She lied when questioned about seeing or knowing about the bracelet. I know what you're thinking, kids lie all the time especially when they're scared. Here's the kicker: When I spoke privately with Shantell, she revealed that her mother was aware of the bracelet all along and instructed her to lie about it. Shantell also mentioned that Mrs. Mason went to the bathroom during our session when she told me all she was going to do was check on her daughter."

"Dr. Whittman, it is common for someone to use the restroom unexpectedly, it frequently happens to me."

"Detective, we are not discussing you at the moment. I am referring to a woman with mental health concerns whom I have been treating. Despite the question, she stayed calm and didn't mention needing the restroom. She hid very important information dealing with my sisters' death. She should be seen as a suspect and further questioned regarding the new information I shared."

"I will follow up tomorrow and visit Mrs. Mason. I'll let you know if the information is credible or just a scared child's imagination. If you don't mind me asking doctor, what have you been treating Mrs. Mason for? I understand the need for confidentiality, but it would provide insight into the type of person I may be dealing with."

"This concerns my sister, so I don't care about the doctor, patient policy, or laws. I'll do whatever it takes to ensure justice for my sister's killer."

"We didn't classify your sister's case as a homicide, but now that we have this new information, I'm willing to delve deeper to determine if the accounts don't align."

"I appreciate it, detective. I'm treating Mrs. Mason for depression and post-traumatic stress disorder. Some have even said that she killed her own son, but I only saw a grieving mother and it wasn't my job to say whether she did or didn't kill her own child, which she denied all allegations. She mentioned her in-laws' dislikes for her, resulting in the spread of falsehoods among their circles. She has been coping with the allegations."

"I think I have enough to reopen the investigation. I will keep you informed of my findings. If you speak to the Masons again, don't mention anything else. Leave the detective work to me. Find out more from their daughter. Children overhear their parent's conversations all the time. There might be something useful. Please provide any discovered information discreetly, as we have enough evidence for an arrest. With Mrs. Mason, I will exercise utmost caution."

"One more thing I forgot to tell you. I mentioned to her husband what his daughter told me."

"Why," asked detective Chase?

"Well, I wanted him to be aware of his wife's deception in case they are in potential danger.

"Have you ever thought that perhaps her husband may be protecting what he himself may already know of his wife allegedly having something to do with your sister's potential murder."

"No, I guess I wasn't thinking of that," exclaimed the doctor.

"That's because you're emotionally tied to this case. Always remember anyone is a potential witness or suspect sorry to say that even includes yourself. So, if you know you're clear of any involvement and want me to proceed with this additional evidence, I will reopen the case and do what's necessary to capture the murderer."

"I have nothing to do with the death of my sister."

Detective Chase agreed, "I'll reach out soon. Stay put and remember, no revealing suspicions to the Masons or the case's reopening. Carry on as usual."

Being awakened he couldn't get back to sleep, detective Chase took a closer look at his notes from previous questions, he asked the Masons and compared them to the new information given to him by Doctor Whittman. He followed up further on Veronica's mental stability by digging further into the death of her son, perhaps autopsy reports may have something that he may be able to connect for a stronger case. Given her mental health concerns, one wonders how the Masons were able to adopt in the first place.

CHAPTER 20

Prime Suspects

Detective Chase made his way to the coroner's office to see if he could get access to the Mason's son's death certificate. Hello, may I help you?" Ask the coroner.

"Perhaps, I'm Detective Chase. I'm here to see if I can obtain a death certificate for a deceased child. Do you recall any records of the Masons? The mother was Veronica Mason, a young boy."

"Ahh sorry detective, we have so many bodies come through here. I can't come close to remembering them all. My presence here has lasted for nearly four decades. The brain isn't as it was.

"Do you have any documentation I could review for potential use? asked detective Chase.

"It's not normal for us to allow anyone to thumb through any personal records, but as a detective, I guess you wouldn't be here if it wasn't important, so yea go-ahead son have at it. Your desired item should be in one of those boxes." The old man giggled upon seeing detective Chase's face, staring at stacks of disorganized papers.

"You must be kidding me," said Detective Chase, overwhelmed before even starting. Hey is there at least a starting point or do I just dive in?"

"Listen, I have work to do. Locate it yourself. Elderly individuals can be quite cantankerous," Chase mused. As detective Chase rummaged through the file, he became weary.

"You haven't found the paperwork you're looking for yet, young man?" asked the coroner.

"Regrettably not, and I'm over it." Detective Chase stated he would need to take a different path. He threw his hands up in the air. The coroner suggested trying the electrical box in the other room.

"What?" asked Detective Chase.

"You're familiar with the small box containing numbers and letters."

"Do you mean a computer?" asked the detective with frustration.

"Yes, that's it, that's what the others called it," relayed the clueless old coroner. You see me, I like paper. You can never go wrong with paper documents.

"Can you tell me why you didn't tell me about the computer hours ago?"

"Guess I forgot," said the old coroner.

"Just show me where the computer is. I hope you have the password.

"Aww yes, no worries. I have it written here somewhere. Let me think I believe it's in my favorite book, KOOSHMA THE ORIGIN. Have you heard of it?" asked the old coroner.

"No, I haven't. I don't have time to hear about it either," exclaimed Detective Chase, tired and frustrated.

"Knowing the origin is key; without it, solving a case is impossible. Let me grab it right fast. I know it's here somewhere, pushing aside other old dusty books before he finds it. Sharing the password, treating the book like valuable artwork. He proceeded, pointing to the password that read KOOSHMA REBORN. "Kooshma Reborn, yes, that's reminding me what the password is for. It serves as a reminder that this is the next book for my collection. Did I mention true events inspired it? Happened to me once, but I whipped that old Kooshma coming for me while I tried taking a nap. Never tried again. I tell you; this old guy has some fights left in him." The elderly coroner, amid his ramblings, realized he had forgotten the detectives' initial question and apologized for his forgetfulness.

"Disregard, I found it. The autopsy findings suggest cradle death, and you were the attending coroner," asked detective Chase.

"I believe if something claims to be, it is. Do you

understand my firm belief, not just in that case, but in others as well?"

"What?" asked the detective.

"KOOSHMA? Yea, he got me, but people just think I'm a senile old man."

"And I'm starting to believe them," laughed the detective. "Okay, I have to go. I spent hours here and found nothing that can help.

"Nice having you," The old man said, "I'll see you soon. Go to the beginning, remember The Origin, everything has a beginning." He stood in the door, shouting to the detective as he drove away.

"Crazy old man," mumbled the detective. What's next? he asked himself. Attempting to provide an answer to a question that would arise. All he heard was the coroner's last words replaying in his head. The beginning, yes, he said to himself. Well Chase, it looks like it's time to take a road trip. Pushing his car to the max, leaving a cloud of dust behind him, speeding beyond the limit.

CHAPTER 21

Family time

Veronica inquired as they lay together, preparing for the night. "That's precisely what we need. I've been lying here, struggling to come up with something positive for us, considering everything we've been through lately. We need to escape and reassess our priorities. I genuinely believe that we've allowed the life we envisioned once the adoption was completed to take a back seat to our priorities."

"Do you mean us as in you and me or as a family, including Shantell?" asked Tom.

"For now, it's just you and me. Shantell still has school." Tom hoped that a change of scenery would help ease some of the tension, especially with the presence of Francine, who he viewed as a potential threat to his marriage.

"Great idea!" Veronica exclaimed, but what about Shantell? I mean, who can we trust to watch her?"

"Tom took a deep breath and exhaled. I know you will not like what I'm about to say…? He…? Hesitating again before blurting out his suggestion, Blair."

"Blair? Your sister?" Her excitement turning into aggravation. "How can you even suggest your sister, knowing how she and I feel about each other?"

"That's just it Veronica, your feelings for Blair are independent of Shantell's. It could be a fresh start for you and her. Remember, with the passing of my mother, Blair is alone. They can bond and keep each other company. Despite her condescending nature, Blair has always shown a strong sense of responsibility, which is why I trust her with our daughter. You forgot she raised me, now look at me. I'm amazing, right?" Laughing out loud, softening the mood to a pleasant one. Finally, they both could agree on asking Blair to watch over Shantell for a few days.

"Hopefully Shantell will feel comfortable with Blair," said Veronica nervously.

"I'm sure she'll be fine. Shantell seems to get along well with anyone. Besides, she understands Blair is family, and I can't wait to see the look on Blair's face when we ask. She has desired this for some time. I think we should hold off for a few days before asking her. Saturday is the day for my mother's cremation, and

I don't want to overwhelm her during this delicate time. Besides, it will give us time to book that retreat we went on for our third anniversary."

"Oh yeah, Elenor's bed-and-breakfast. Veronica, with a satisfied expression, described it as a magnificent, peaceful spot in the middle of nowhere.

"Then it's decided, we will discuss it with Shantell tomorrow before I bring her to school," said Tom. Standing at the edge of the bed the next morning just staring at Tom and Veronica sleep was Dabria. Imagine the ease of taking lives as they lie there. Her yearning for her power grew as she realized she had given them up in exchange for limited control over her life as a human. Amid her slumber, Veronica shifts to her other side. As she shifted positions in her sleep, Dabria came into view on the edge of her vision.

"Shantell, honey, what are you doing standing there? It's 4 am," Veronica whispered. "You have a few hours left before waking up for school."

"I'm not tired anymore. Could you make me some waffles for breakfast?" asked Shantell.

"Shantell, I'm exhausted," her mom said wearily.

"Dad, can you make them for me? asked Dabria. Tom was completely asleep, snoring so loudly that he couldn't hear her, completely unaware of the world around him. Fine, I can do it myself, but next time I ask, I bet you won't ask me to do it myself again, Dabria thought to herself. With a clear agenda behind her thinking. With a resolute mindset, Dabria set the toaster to maximum power, fully intending to leave the waffles inside until the recommended time was up. Understanding that simply burning the waffles wouldn't generate a substantial disturbance, Dabria altered her approach and poured water into the toaster, resulting in an electrical fire erupting. Awakened by the fire alarm opening the door to a smoke-filled house, Mason's primary concern was Shantell.

"Shantell! screamed Tom. Shantell, where are you?" Tom yelled again. He searched her room first, forgetting that he had told her to fix breakfast. In a rush, Tom dashed to the bathroom after not hearing anything from her. Veronica suddenly remembered that Shantell had asked for waffles. Veronica's voice echoed through the house.

"Tom, check the kitchen! Rushing downstairs, Tom twisted his ankle, pushing through. Despite the pain in his ankle, Tom rushed to the kitchen, deftly moving Dabria out of the way, and swiftly grabbed the fire extinguisher hidden beneath the kitchen sink, successfully extinguishing the fire. Veronica ran to Dabria.

"Shantell, are you ok? Honey, are you hurt?"

"I'm ok, I just tried to make breakfast like you told me." Tom wanted to question Veronica's decision to allow Shantell to make her own breakfast without supervision. In the aftermath, all he remembered was Shantell near the fire. not moving an inch or panicking. Why hadn't she moved to warn them about the fire? He saw her just standing there, appearing to be mesmerized by the flames.

"Thank goodness you're ok honey, you could have burned down the entire house," said Veronica nervously.

'Sorry mommy, is it my fault?

"No, I didn't get up when you asked. Tom, how about you? Are you ok? I heard you stumble while rushing downstairs."

"I'm fine. My ankle is twisted. It's just sore right now. Thank God, I made it in time to put out the fire. It only spread to a portion of the kitchen wall before I extinguished it, but it looks like a complete remodel of that section. You'll get what you've always wanted sooner. Let's open some doors and windows." Tom, this getaway was perfectly timed.

"Getaway, where are we going? Dabria said, sounding eager.

"Let's leave this smoky place. Maybe the smoke hasn't affected our clothes. We can get dressed and continue the start of our near-death experience"

Laughing out loud to keep from crying. They all hurried upstairs to change into their clothes and then left the house.

"Veronica, can you drop me off at work after we drop Shantell at school?

Veronica said, "Sure and I will contact Howard's remodeling to give us an estimate of the damage. He can provide us with a deal considering all the business we gave them, not counting the referrals. Now let's pull the Band-Aid off. Shantell, your dad and I are planning a getaway for a few days. Since you still have school, we will ask Aunt Blair if she can watch you for a while. How do you feel about that?"

"It doesn't matter to if you guys want to leave me, especially after what I did this morning. I don't blame you." As expected, Dabria took advantage of Shantell's emotional turmoil and remained unaffected by their departure.

"No honey, it's not like that. We planned ongoing before the incident this morning. As we explained to you before, that was our fault. We shouldn't have allowed you to handle that type of responsibility. In fact, the wiring needed to be fixed, anyway. I think I remember now that I had problems with that toaster, but I forgot about it."

Despite it being a complete fabrication, Veronica attempted to prevent Shantell from feeling guilty. Tom understood the hidden meaning and played the game. "So, Shantell, do you mind staying with Aunt Blair? After I ask her and she agrees, which I'm sure she will. Spending time with you is something she's been longing for."

"Yeah, I understand, Dad," Dabria acknowledged. "Things could change," she pondered silently.

"Then it's settled," said Tom. I will check with Blair and let you guys know when it's set in stone. We're here, See you after school.

In the distance, Francine stood like clockwork. She attempted to stop Tom's car to inform him about the counseling session she had with Shantell, who she thought was the innocent ten-year-old that walked through the school doors months ago. Spotting Veronica in the car, she refrained from approaching and opted to wait for a different opportunity, as her cell phone was now rendered useless. He would have to answer the phone if it was the school calling. Considering the perfect time to call without Veronica. Alone again, Francine would deem it the opportune moment to make the call. The school bell rang, the race to reach class intensified, with Mrs. Clemens reminding everyone there to hurry before the doors shut. Dabria arrived at her desk on time and noticed Melanie seated a few seats away, as expected after their previous meeting. Raving on about death wasn't the conversation that has friends gravitating towards you. Mrs. Clemens, familiar with children frequently having minor disagreements and swiftly resuming their play, opted not to bring it up.

"Now, class, a few weeks ago, I had each one of you write a poem as a class assignment. Just so you know, the poems are in the state poetry contest. The best written works came down to two students whom I will have read in front of the class today and everyone else will vote for the one poem who they think should represent the school, and don't forget that you are all beautiful and remarkable students. The best written work was done by Shantell Mason and Adam Hayes."

Dabria was taken aback, she suddenly realized that she had been dormant within Shantell. The class erupted into applause, except for Melanie, who purposely avoided any interaction with Dabria.

"Class, settle down. I have your poems. Whoever

wants to go first, let's start reading. Then we'll vote in secret. So, who's first?" asked Mrs. Clemens? Adam's courteous behavior showed a deliberate strategy of allowing the ladies to go before him. What a gentleman," said Mrs. Clemens. "Shantell you may come up here, grab your poem and begin."

Dabria was confident in her ability to handle this. My only task is to read Shantell's words. "The title of the poem is called Monstrous Feelings. Our feelings can be very confusing, like big scary monsters that stomp and roar, joy, sadness, anger, and fear. That's what makes us. Feelings can be a blissful moment, or they can make our hearts sink. We can feel elated and scared of the full spectrum of our entire body. However, there are hidden things beyond our sight. It lurks there underneath the surface a feeling called anxiety. It starts off quiet and hard to see, but with time, it increases in size, taunting us, sticking to us like glue, causes chaos, worry, and distress. It prevents us from finding joy and can cause us stress. But no need to be afraid. Yelling won't make it go away. All it needs is a kind hand. The warmth of light or a flame. Avoid staring but try to know it. Try to know what causes its pain. And when we get to know it, the less power it has. The things that drive it. What makes it calm, putting it to rest. Although the feeling is monstrous, it doesn't have to feel so strong. It's ok to have it in our lives as an emotional part of us making it our own. Find a way to cope. Fighting makes it worse. Anxiety can be overwhelming and terrifying. A feeling without change, but I promise if you let release it, you may surprise yourself. So, reach out and let someone hear your thoughts and feelings. Speak about it and keep trying to find ways to get along with that monstrous feeling."

Dabria met Mrs. Clemens with a piercing gaze as she poured her heart and soul into understanding the poem, suddenly realized that Shantell had penned verses about her own life. Dabria, a feeling that she struggled to tame, eventually finding solace in the art of poetry, personified Shantell's anxiety. The applause filled the room, with even Melanie joining in, believing that she now comprehended Shantell's behavior and could offer her more supportive friendship. Dabria wore a dry smile as she made her way back to her desk, while Melanie moved back to her assigned seat behind Dabria.

"Shantell, that was a great poem, you're sure to win. You have my vote. Adam can't possibly compete with that," said Melanie." In fact, you should be proud of yourself, no matter who wins."

"Quiet down class," yelled Mrs. Clemens. "Shantell, that was wonderful. Although challenging, Adam will now speak."

Showing no signs of nervousness, Adam strode confidently towards the front of the class to recite his poem. Adam, who's usually a class clown, became focused. "The passing of my cousin inspired me to write this." Adam cleared his throat before he began "ahem". "My poem is called, 'Forever a king'. "I was conceived to be someone successful, a king among kings. First, I had to become a son, cousin, brother, nephew, and grandson. Check one accomplished, having a family of my own, having children, the thing my family of established kings and queens foreseen as part of my future, stolen. Although I haven't achieved father or husband status. I still achieved the crown of a king by default. The streets robbed me of chances; a place where I was warned not to stay, unfit for royalty. Naysayers missed it as street gatekeepers silently spread the mess through the unlocked back door. I looked ahead, trusting right actions would protect me. Gatekeepers, I see you and I know you know. I also witness your tears when you receive that phone call in the middle of the night, informing you that someone has taken away your king or queen forever. I wish this for nobody; I could have been greater. The pain in my family will never die, as I watch from heaven. I wasn't the only one you hurt. My family mourns the one that has seen nothing when your eyes are wide open. You and yours could be next. Those same ones robbed me of greatness. Remember me always!! and finally to my family worry no more. I'm safe now, walking through heaven's doors where I never have to watch my back ever again. I'm at peace and have taken my place with all mighty God, the true king of kings."

The entire classroom was hushed, their eyes fixed on the tear-streaked face of Adam. Moments later, the children erupted into applause, rising to their feet. While the rest of the class erupted in applause, Mrs. Clemens stayed seated, understanding the depth of emotion in Adam's words.

"Calm down everyone and take your seats, it's time to vote. You can only vote once. I will pass the box around with some sticky notes to write down your favorite poem," said Mrs. Clemens. Keep in mind, the person chosen will represent the school for the district finals.

As their turn to vote approached, every student in the class thoughtfully considered their feelings towards each poem, concealing their answers with care. Mrs. Clemens, full of enthusiasm, collected the box and carried it to her desk, curious about the outcome of the votes.

"Everyone, sit quietly so I can tally up the votes. "Just a moment," said Mrs. Clemens. Disregarding Mrs. Clemens' hope for a swift resolution, the class exchanged whispers, safeguarding their votes to prevent any potential social isolation resulting from their choices. Mrs. Clemens tried to quiet the class, her voice rising above the hushed murmurs.

"I have the count for each poem read by Adam and Shantell. No matter the result, you should all take pride in yourselves. It was very close and both poems were amazing. I wish that both of you could represent us with your beautiful written work. However, Adam will be the school's representative."

The class gathered around Adam to congratulate him. He walked up to Dabria with an extended hand. "I loved your poem Shantell," said Adam. He pulled her in a little closer and whispered into her ear. "We both knew you didn't have a chance of beating me," Adam boasted.

Dabria became enraged not because of losing the poetry votes, but because she could care less. The boasting ignited her malice, squeezing Adam's hand even harder than he did hers. He struggled to have his hand released, rubbing it for relief afterwards. The bells tintinnabulation rose over the chattering noise of the students to be released for recess. Dabria trailed Adam and his companions, plotting her opportunity for retaliation. Dabria recklessly bumped into Francine as she was called by Dabria, now speaking on a first name basis, which she easily got away with through blackmail and deception.

"Well, hello," Francine said with a sneer.

"Shantell, I don't know what type of games you're playing, but you're a child trying to enter an adult business, and that's nowhere you aspire to be, especially with me. Psychology is my specialty, among other collective attributes," Francine declared confidently.

Dabria laughed uproariously. "You know, I think I'm ready to end you, Francine." Francine backed away slowly with fear making sure not to show weakness. "Bye Francine," said Dabria. I know we will bump into each other again, next time hopefully it doesn't have to be in such public settings. One thing you said was correct Francine I will admit I don't know you, but I promise, you don't want to know me."

CHAPTER 22

Explaining the unexplainable

Detective Chase reached the spot where the Masons supposedly adopted Shantell, he found himself perplexed by the presence of a deserted structure. As he stepped out of his vehicle, he noticed the intact sign of Mrs. Flackman's orphanage, which contrasted with the abandoned and partially burned structure that no one had touched for several months, if not years. Detective Chase said to himself "Correct location but lacks logic. It's just not possible." Despite the belief that it was impossible, he resolved to explore the wreckage, hoping to find a clue for his next step.

The detective's heart sank, sensing dread in the

desolate building, stepping on remnants of a haunting catastrophe. He meticulously searched through every room, his heart skipped a beat when he stumbled upon a file room that lay in ruins, reduced to ashes. Among the unreadable papers, he stumbled upon fragments of Shantell's file, revealing her adoptive last name, Segura. Among the papers that were still legible, he found fragments of Shantell's file, revealing a glimpse into the adoption homes she had lived in and a dimly visible psychiatric report.

Patient #176, Shantell Segura, frequently moves between foster families. She has had two failed adoptions, which ended in heartbreaking tragedies involving the parents of the adoptees. Patient #176, who is diagnosed with multiple personality disorder, created a stronger personality as a coping mechanism to mask her feelings. I have encountered another persona named Dabria. Her demeanor suggests a complete lack of empathy, hinting at a capacity for unspeakable acts. Detective Chase, his face filled with worry, read the final fragile page that disintegrated in his grasp, concerned for the safety of the Masons and all those connected to Shantell's life.

Day 17, Shantell and I had a normal conversation, a conversation one would have with any average 10-year-old, but things changed. She attacked me with my letter opener. I asked her questions about the death of her former adoptive homes, all of which had unanswered deaths except for a few words from the one surviving father of the last adoptees. Even though they found the mother dead and Shantell's father unconscious, they claimed Shantell was at school and did not experience a life-threatening amount of exposure. However, the dad, who is still alive, remains in a coma at Lakefront hospital. I'm hoping to get more answers from him as soon as he regains consciousness 'if he ever regains consciousness.

The unsettling events surrounding the first family's fatal exposure to chemical fumes and the subsequent tragedies involving the second family have left me with a multitude of questions following my encounter with Dabria. Startled by a noise downstairs, Detective Chase swiftly stashed the salvageable papers regarding Shantell's diagnosis in his pockets. As the sun began to set, he heard strange sounds that became more pronounced the longer he stayed in the building perhaps rodents scurrying or remnants falling he thought. "Let me get out of here." Desperate to leave, detective Chase encountered a suspicious gray-haired bearded man snooping around his vehicle.

"Hey, what are you doing?" Yelled Detective Chase.

The man was startled and backed away. "Sorry, I'm not used to anyone visiting this old place." Said the gray-haired man. I'm usually the only one dwelling through this old building. I've been visiting this place regularly for years.

"Really?" asked detective Chase. Tell me about what took place here. Sorry for not introducing myself. I'm Detective Chase. I'm here for case follow-up."

Noticing the license plate, the man remarked, "You're not from here, are you?"

"Very observant Mr. Chase. Retired detective Segura, Mr. Chase.

"Wow, what are the chances of two detectives searching the same area?" said Chase.

"I'm sure for different reasons. My reasons are because I lost someone that once was important to me who died here during the explosion that destroyed this orphanage," said Segura. I gave my niece up for adoption when my sister died from cancer. My condition then hindered effective care for her. I was indulging in heavy drinking and had to go through periods of rehab. The horrors I witnessed exceed anything nightmares can conjure."

"Wait a minute, did you say your name is Segura?"

"Yes, why?"

"Was the child you gave up for adoption a boy or girl?"

"A girl named Shantell," he said.

"This is crazy Mr. Segura. I came seeking information about a little girl adopted from here nearly a year ago.

Segura stood there, speechless." It can't be," said Segura. Could you describe the girl?

"Her distinct features include being a ten-year-old African American girl with an unexpected head of white hair."

"Wait, what's going on Chase?" Your describing the girl I gave up for adoption, are you claiming that she's alive." Detective Chase, Shantell died in that fire. I identified her body myself and she couldn't have come from this orphanage months ago because it was just as you see it now."

"Segura, you're talking crazy. I saw Shantell myself, and I know the people that adopted her. Are they in danger Segura? Should I call and warn the Masons?

No time now! Do you think you can take me to her? Fear fills my heart, not just for the Masons, but for everyone she encounters. I should have killed her when she was born.

"You mean kill Shantell? How could you? Could you tell me why you would think about killing your own niece? asked Detective Chase.

"She really isn't my niece I will explain later."

Detective Chase questioned himself, unsure if he should trust the words of someone who appeared delusional. Based on the files, he inclined to believe him. "Segura, I will take you to her. The Masons aren't picking up, but there's no way I will allow you to harm the girl," exclaimed Detective Chase.

"The mistakes I made with her as a baby have returned to haunt me," said Segura. We must leave immediately."

CHAPTER 23

Don't call me Shantell

"Tom, I can't believe we're going to the place where we spent our honeymoon. "It's as if we're getting married all over again," said Veronica.

"I know, I'm just sorry that it took so long. Maybe we could turn this into a yearly tradition. What do you think?

"Come on, stop playing! Do you think Shantell will handle us being away, especially doing this yearly."

"She didn't appear to mind. Do you think she will miss us? I mean, I know Blair can call us if she has any issues, but I'm feel much better knowing I left my phone with Shantell."

"By allowing Shantell to contact us, we can spare your sister from constant inconvenience whenever she wants to reach us, and we can also safeguard our peaceful retreat from incessant phone disruptions."

"Well, we have another hour before we get to the air BNB. Contact her to ensure everything's alright and bring peace of mind to both of you."

"I think you're right. Let me try calling Blair. Tom, the phone is just ringing. She might be busy. What time is it? Shantell should have left school by now."

"Try calling my phone to see if she picks up."

"Hello?" Dabria answered after the second ring.

"Hi honey, this is Mom. I called to see how everything was going with Aunt Blair."

"Everything is going well. Aunt Blair and I are having an amazing time already. Last night we played hide and seek. Then I made up a new game that she likes called dump the trash."

"Dump the trash?" asked Veronica. "How do you play that?"

"It's about finding things that don't belong. Dabria had dissected Blair's body with a kitchen knife.

Covered in her blood, Oblivious to the gruesome murder she had committed, Tom and Veronica chatted on the speakerphone, unaware of Dabria's meticulous dissection of Blair's limbs which resulted in an atrocious death.

"That's exceptional," said Veronica. Hitting it off after just one day. I'm glad honey, make sure you keep up with your schoolwork as well.

"I will, don't worry Veronica," said Dabria. Briefly slipping out of her disposition.

"What? Veronica asked, "What?" Did you call me by my name? What happened to calling me mommy?"

"Sorry mom, I was trying to figure out this math problem."

Veronica put her hand over her chest. "Oh good, I was worried there for a minute. I thought we were heading backwards with our progress because we left, and you didn't want to admit it."

"No, that's not it. I'm just thinking about this multiplication problem."

"Ask Aunt Blair for help!" yelled Tom. Can she hear me, honey? Put it on the speakerphone so I can speak to her. Where is she? Your mom tried calling her phone a while ago, and she didn't answer."

Stumbling momentarily, Dabria managed to find an excuse. "Aunt Blair is out in the yard, speaking to some guy. She has been there for a while.

"Um hum, I wonder if my sister finally started dating," replied Tom. It's been a while since she has invited anyone into her life so easily, given how her last relationship ended. Well honey, your mom and I are about to pull up to the Air BnB tell Aunt Blair that we called and if she needs to, call your mom's phone. And if you absolutely need to speak to us honey, you can call at any time. But your mom or I will call you every day to check on you. Until tomorrow, we love you."

"Love you too," murmured Dabria. The thin bags began to burst as Dabria tried to stuff Blair's severed corpse into each one, pieces at a time. Contemplating, she was convinced of a better solution. Frustrated with the results, she discarded the dismembered pieces and explore a different approach. Dabria took out Tom's phone and began to text.

"Hey Francine, can you meet me at my sister's house? We need to talk. My sister isn't home right now, so we can speak openly."

"I was told that you were out of town," Francine responded.

Dabria continued the conversation through the text. Veronica went ahead of me. I will meet her there. I had to see a client. Meet me in an hour. I will send you the address."

"Good, Dabria's voice trembled as she whispered, "I have to grieve another loss." Crafting a ploy, she enticed Francine into a trap, leaving her completely unaware of the impending danger awaiting her at Blair's home. Francine couldn't resist the fabricated text from Dabria, as two pressing matters occupied her thoughts. The upcoming meeting with Tom occupied her thoughts. Another aspect was that she planned to share her suspicions about Shantell with him. Her emotions for Tom made her believe there was an opportunity for their connection to move forward. Beyond a simple kiss, she wanted more.

Francine made it to Blairs home for she and Toms rendezvous, gently opening the door she peeked her head inside. "Hello?" Francine heard a voice and saw the house in near-total darkness. The feeble rays of the streetlights found their way through the slight opening in the window blinds, providing the sole source of light in the otherwise darkened house. She anxiously scanned the dimly lit living room for a light switch.

"Tom!" yelled Francine.

The intensity of her yell filled the entire house, showing her terror and triggering an accelerated heart rate. Francine grabbed her phone to dial Tom's number. In the distance, she heard the ringing of his phone. The ring led her to the back of the house dropping her phone in the process. As it collided with the hardwood floor, her phone's screen cracked.

"Damn!" exclaimed Francine.

Panicked, Francine dropped to the ground, urgently rummaging around for her phone. Her fingers navigated the sticky, wet ground until they landed on her phone. With the phone in hand, she illuminated the room, giving it a reddish tint. The realization that it was blood sent a chilling feeling through Francine. To her horror, Francine stumbled upon Blair's decapitated head, whose cold, vacant gaze was directed towards her just a few feet ahead. Francine's panicked shriek echoed through the silence.

"Tom!" she yelled again. Fearing he might be in danger as well. In a state of panic, she hurled herself towards the door, losing her balance and crashing onto the floor, her feet slipping on the coagulating blood. Just as she was about to escape outside, the door slammed shut, locking her inside. The sound of dogs barking filled the air all at once. They heard the sirens of police cars before they could even turn the corner. Dabria made a call from a neighbor's house from around the corner. Arriving at their home, imposing as a terrified ten-year-old girl that escaped a deranged killer, she had murdered her aunt without being detected. Armed and prepared, the police shouted for anyone inside to exit with hands raised before forcefully entering the residence. Terrified and covered in blood, Francine burst out of Blair's home as soon as the door swung open.

The sound of gunshots filled the air as the police officers reacted to the alarming situation, abruptly ending Francine's life. A disturbed young girl provided the only remaining account of the incident. Resulting in everyone questioning the motives behind Francine's atrocious act. The loud ring of Veronica's phone startled her, and Tom and they instinctively felt a sense of dread knowing that a call at 4 am could only bring bad news.

"Hello?" answered Veronica.

"Hi, is this the Masons' number?"

"Yes,

"Mrs. Mason this is Sergeant Rideau. I need you to make it to Ms. Blair Mason's home as soon as possible."

"Could you tell me why what's wrong? Tom, something's wrong?"

"Is it Shantell?" asked Tom.

"I don't know. Sergeant, is my daughter, ok?"

"Sorry Mrs. Mason, I can't divulge that information over the phone. How soon can you make it here?"

"In about 3 hours." Tom had already gotten dressed and started packing without hesitation.

"Tell you what." Just come to precinct 35 when you get to town, and we will explain everything," said sergeant Rideau.

"Please sergeant, can you at least tell me if my little girl is, ok?"

"Yes, she's ok. She'll be here with us at the station, talk to you then, Mrs. Mason."

CHAPTER 24

Not my little girl

After explaining the story about Shantell's background, Detective Chase became even more skeptical.

"I must admit, Mr. Segura, your story sounds outlandish, but from what you told me, I can't disregard the threat to people's lives," said Detective Chase. And from the files I showed you concerning Shantell, you may be right. The therapist at the adoption agency had questions himself. But calling it supernatural is unlikely."

"Detective Chase, how would you explain adopting a child from a nonexistent agency? I can't shake the concern that lingers within me regarding this multiple personality illness. Upon reaching her, we will uncover the actual answers we seek. She is dangerous. And with further reevaluation, when I take her into custody, we can close this case.

It explains a lot, though. Since the Masons brought Shantell into their lives, there have been quite a few unsolved murders that's circulating around the Mason family. A little girl's death at a sleepover was ruled negligence by the manufacturer. The authorities ruled the therapist sister's death, while monitoring Shantell, as suicide. Until the deceased sister, Dr. Whittman, brought it to my attention. Shantell, or should I say Dabria, pointed us in her mother's direction.

"As I have previously mentioned, detective Chase Dabria has been projected. She must be killed," exclaimed Segura. "Something I should have done when she was born. Her abilities are beyond your comprehension. We may have a chance if she has gotten what she wants."

"And what is that asked Segura?"

"To be reincarnated into the complete human form. She has lived for centuries. That's the only way she can lift the curse bestowed upon her that has blackened her heart, to the point where there's nothing left inside of her that can survive."

"Let's just say I entertain the notion that everything you're saying is true. I can't let you kill a kid, Segura, not on my watch."

"Fine, just call whomever you must and warn them. Because the devil has entered their lives and is near. I'll call Mrs. Mason now. The phone rang and Veronica picks up. "Hel – lo, hello Mrs. Mason. Can you hear me?" screamed detective Chase?

"Detective is th-at y-ou. The phone must be in a poor area", yelled Veronica.

"Mrs. Mason, you and your husband may be in danger. It's Shantell. It's hard to explain, but she may not be Shantell, she has split personalities.

"Detective, I can't understand anything you're saying. If you can hear me, we're heading to the precinct now. See you in an hour."

"Mrs. Mason, Mrs. Mason, don't hang up, you're in danger. In a fit of desperation, Detective Chase flung his phone against the dashboard. Shit, she hung up and I don't think she heard anything I said. She mentioned heading to the precinct and meeting me there. What do you think happened?" asked Detective Chase.

"Honestly? Dabria occurred, and I believe exceeding the speed limit is necessary. Push the car to its limit. The scent of burning rubber invaded the vehicle as Detective Chase pressed hard on the accelerator, propelling the car well past the legal speed limit and close to ninety miles per hour.

"Can you text them? Do you think they will receive that," asked Segura?

"It depends on their location, most likely rural. They estimate it takes an hour to reach the precinct, but they live just fifteen minutes away. They'll receive the warning once they have reception and a stronger signal."

"Is Shantell with them?" asked Segura.

"I'm not sure. Let me see if I can contact Dr. Whittman, said detective Chase. She might reach them first and possibly explain if I can persuade her to believe any of this. Chase called Dr. Whittman, who picked up on the first ring."

"Detective Chase? answered Dr. Whittman. I have been waiting for you to call. Do you have any answers about my sister? Did you question Veronica yet?"

"No, I didn't, Doc. Listen. Something else came up and I didn't get to question her. When Chase attempted to provide an explanation, Dr. Whittman cut him off.

"What, why? You're the one I thought I could trust to catch my sister's killer, and you're not even concerned about the case, even with evidence I gave you. I solved the case for you, Dr. Whittman granted, without pausing."

"Dr. Whittman, if you would shut up, I can explain everything," Chase shouted. Dr. Whittman's voice was abruptly hushed. What I've been working on has everything to do with your sister's case. But it has taken a weird turn and after I explain the important details, you may think I'm crazy. You need an open mind right now."

"Ok detective, I'm listening, in my profession being open-minded is mandatory. After providing the doctor with a detailed explanation, he omitted any mention of the supernatural elements as they appeared irrelevant. Dr. Whittman was in aww.

"You're telling me that Shantell has an alter ego

named Dabria that has the potential to kill and may have killed my sister?" asked Dr. Whittman. "I mean, it's possible," said Dr. Whittman.

"So, you believe me? Listen, I need you to go to the police station and warn the Masons, explain it to them as detailed as you can. They may not believe you because it's their daughter, but you have to make them. Stall them until I get there and Doc, be careful. Veronica and Tom had already made it to the police station before receiving the text from Detective Chase and Dr. Whittman's multiple missed phone calls. In a rush to make it to Shantell, Veronica's phone had fallen from her purse and slid between the car seats. In panic, Tom and Veronica rushed into the building to find Shantell talking with a police counselor.

"Tom, there she is!" exclaimed Veronica. Feeling a little less anxious as she ran to Dabria. Honey are you ok?" asked Veronica.

What happened? "Tom asked the counselor." And are you, her parents?

"Yes," Veronica answered. Well, sorry I can't divulge any information. You will have to talk to the lead detectives.

"And where can I find them? "Tom asked?

"Go left, his office is three doors down. He should be in there. Shantell, why don't you stay here while your parents speak to the detective," said the counselor.

"Can you tell me why our daughter can't come with us? asked Veronica.

"Mrs. Mason, considering everything that has

happened. I believe it's best that she stays here for now. She has been through a lot today and hearing the details of what happened tonight all over again will probably be even more damaging"

"Shantell, where is your aunt Blair?" asked Tom?

Dabria looked up at Tom and cried meaningless tears, increasing her narcissistic behavior. "As I mentioned, it has been a tiring day for her. It's best if you guys speak to the detective without her. His name is Davis."

Fine, honey, where not going far? We will be right back stay here with...? Sorry we didn't get your name. "It's Sharon," answered the counselor. Stay here with Sharon, your mother and I will be right back.

Tom and Veronica spotted the name tag on Detective Davis's door and knocked. During a call, Detective Davis yelled for them to come in. "I'll call you back, love you to," said Davis before hanging up the phone. "How can I help you?" asked Davis.

"The counselor Sharon suggested we meet regarding the situation with our daughter, Shantell. I apologize for my demeanor," said Tom.

"Your Shantell's parents."

"Yes, answered Tom. What Happened?"

"Sit down, both of you," advised the detective. Early this morning, we received a phone call stating that there was an incident that happened at the home of Ms. Blair Mason.

"Yes, that's my sister," said Tom. She was babysitting our daughter while we were out of town"

"Sorry, I regret to inform you we found Ms. Blair Mason murdered inside her home after we intercepted an assailant who was trying to escape when we got there."

Tom's knees became weak causing him to almost collapse on the floor. Veronica offered her support by wrapping her arm around Tom, consoling him in his time of need. "Sorry for your loss," said Detective Davis. The lady who killed your sister met a fatal gunshot. Luckily, your daughter got out safely and was able to find help. Because of that brave little girl in there, we could identify Francine Sanchez, a teacher that worked at your daughter's school as the killer."

"Yes," answered Veronica in disbelief. But I don't understand. Can you explain her motivation for doing this? asked Veronica. What issues could she have with Blair? Tom, do you have any ideas?"

Despite his sincere grief, he used his sadness as a shield against speaking up. No, nothing I can think of," answered Tom." Can I see my sister?

"I hesitate to inform you that the body is in an unfit condition for viewing. Detective Davis suggested, "I have a facial photo that can be used to formally identify her, and I advise against going to the home until you're ready to handle what you will see."

"Let's go Tom," said Veronica.

"Shantell, it's time to leave now," said Tom.

"Thanks for taking such good care of my little girl, Sharon," said Veronica.

"No problem, it was my pleasure, she was such an

angel. Here take my card and reach out for anything, even just to talk."

On the car ride home, Veronica was at a loss for words. Tom had just lost his only remaining family member to violence. "Tom, I'm speechless. Even though Blair and I had our differences, I would never wish this upon her. I thank God that Shantell got out. I can't bear the idea that our little girl may have been killed also. Losing one child was enough."

"I know, I can't believe she's gone. I'm so lucky to have you and Shantell in my life. Otherwise, I don't know what I would do," said Tom. Once we reach home, there is something I need to talk to you about. I don't want Shantell to overhear us."

"What is it? Is it that bad when you can't speak about it in front of our daughter? Does it involve Francine? I could tell from the way you reacted when you heard her name mentioned. I'm not stupid," exclaimed Veronica.

"When I said we won't discuss it now, I meant it. Despite what you may think, things haven't been easy. I have shown my commitment not only to our marriage, but also to this family. Veronica remained quiet. She could only imagine Tom's further thoughts. For someone to kill the person closest to you and call it nothing was an understatement, she thought to herself. They heard the phone ringing soon as they exited their vehicle, but it wasn't of importance now.

"I'm going to put Shantell to bed," said Tom. I will meet you in a few minutes so we can talk. He walked Dabria to her bedroom. Kissed her as usual, tucking her in securely, wishing that he could wipe all the images from her head. Your life was supposed to be better. Meant to be a better home. Overwhelmed by emotion, Tom whispered "wow" as he looked at the face of his little girl, crying not just for losing his sister but also for the pain he had caused his family. "I'm sorry, Shantell," Tom said to Dabria before exiting her room.

The persistent beeping of the answering machine intensified in its aggravation. In a fit of anger, Veronica resorted to tearing the phone wires out of the wall as her only source of relief. She paid no attention to the incessantly blinking light on the answering machine and the pile of 15 unheard messages, eagerly expecting the opportunity to confront Tom about the secrets he had been keeping from her.

"Please, have a seat, Veronica," said Tom, motioning towards an empty chair. He sat next to her and took a deep breath. I've always been by your side, trying to understand and provide the support you needed, even when you pushed me away. I'm not looking for an excuse to give you only facts. A few months ago, as you know, I was the one interacting with most of Shantell's teachers and her activities. Francine was a counselor. She noticed my need for support and how involved I was in Shantell's life. Aware of my marital status, she understood my lingering loneliness. I used the multiple engagements that I had with Francine at first as healing. I mean, she was a counselor and understood where I was coming from with my concerns as a husband and you as a wife.

Veronica, overwhelmed with emotions, refrained from speaking, not letting her anger consume her. Instead, she allowed Tom to conclude his thoughts, yearning for closure and the chance to rebuild their relationship after this unsettling conversation. I'm not sure if you remember the night I came in late. A few weeks ago, at 2:00 am on that very night, I stumbled upon Doctor Whittman's sister's bracelet in your car.

To clarify, it was the night I dropped off Shantell for the sleepover. That night, your car broke down. I could have awakened you to get me. You didn't ask, and I didn't tell, easing my conscience. I used that time to call Francine to come and pick me up. I used it as an excuse to have more than just words and a ride. Although I didn't sleep with her, we kissed. Not sleeping with her isn't an excuse. Putting into place for the possibility for it to happen is where I faltered. And for that, I apologize. I hope for your forgiveness. If not, I understand. I'll try my hardest to make it right. Tom's eyes remained locked on Veronica, anticipating her words or any visible expression, yet she remained unresponsive. The events may have been too fresh in her mind to elicit a response. It's possible that the weight of the situation hadn't sunk in. From her bed upstairs, Dabria sat with a mischievous grin, reveling in her successful execution of yet another malicious scheme, pondering who her next target would be.

CHAPTER 25

Retribution

As Veronica and Tom continued to sleep, Dabria wandered through the house, observing their disregard for the unattended messages on the answering machine. With unsettling events in their community, Dabria found the lack of phone calls strange. Curiosity got the best of her, interested her in pressing the play button on the recorder. Detective Chase took the necessary precautions by incorporating a discreet beep before the first message played, in case Dabria was nearby. Tom or Veronica, I need you to pick up the phone if you're home. Please pick up the phone. It's important. Are you there?

The first message was a series of beeps, followed by Detective Chase leaving identical messages except for the last one, which was left by Doctor Whittman. Tom and Veronica, listen. I need to talk about Shantell. She may not be who you think she is. She asked me to contact you to warn you Shantell had extensive psychological damage while she was in the orphanage. Detective Chase informed me that Shantell has multiple personalities, one of which you already know as the sweet little girl you came to love, and the other goes by the name of Dabria. The part of Dabria that is hurt is the one you know. She's always there for the weaker part of Shantell, who may cease to exist.

Upstairs, the sound of rattling caught Dabria's attention, suggesting that Tom and Veronica were stirring. She cleared the answering machine of any messages. It's time for me to make my move. Sorry mom sorry dad, it's time for Shantell to find a new family, Dabria said to herself. Dabria walked towards Veronica's secret hiding place, the spot where she always stored her medication.

Let me check to see if there's enough clonazepam for one person. Maybe I should ask Dad if he wants some fresh orange juice for breakfast, thought Dabria. Understanding that Tom would be a more challenging individual to approach, Dabria concentrated on him, as he was the only one in the household who drank orange juice. Her go-to beverage was apple juice, considering her allergic reaction to orange juice. Dabria knew that crushing clonazepam tablets and her mom's duloxetine would suffice. Just adequate to induce everlasting sleep.

Tom and Veronica came downstairs, greeting Shantell with a good morning. They noticed she was already awake and asked why she didn't wake them. Aware of her hunger, Veronica inquired about how she slept.

"I slept alright, but I woke up early because I had a vivid and unsettling dream of Miss Sanchez brutally killing Aunt Blair."

To protect Tom's fragile state, the detectives chose not to reveal the details that surrounded the gruesome murder of his sister. Dabria's actions were calculated and intentional. Witnessing Tom drink a small portion of juice, in the anticipation that it would yield the intended result.

"I'm not feeling so well," said Tom. His eyes gradually closed before dropping to the floor.

"Oh my God, Tom, what's wrong? Tom! Veronica shouted. She shifted his attention towards Dabria, who stood still with the knife concealed behind her back, wearing a malevolent smile.

"Shantell, what are you doing? I said get the phone and dial 911 now!"

"Is something wrong with your dad?"

"Now!" Veronica screamed.

With a sinister voice, Dabria replied. "Can you explain wanting to save a cheating man's life?"

"What?" asked Veronica.

"Why are you talking to me like that?

"I overheard the entire conversation that the two of you had. All his lies you believed. Did you think there were no legitimate instances of infidelity" exclaimed Dabria. You are so naïve and don't worry about Tom. I don't think he'll be waking up anytime soon."

Trying to escape, Veronica's nerves got the best of hers, causing her to fumble with the chain on the latch of the front door. Dabria seized this opportunity to slice her wrist, ensuring that she remained confined within the house. Desperate to elude Dabrias venery, Veronica sprinted towards the top of the stairs, but Dabria caught her shirt. In their struggle, Veronica's strength proved superior, but she couldn't escape being pulled down the stairs by Dabria. Their violent journey down the stairs resulted in a series of bone-crushing sounds, with Veronica's arm and Dabria's leg succumbing to the force before their bodies collided at the staircase's base, the knife embedding itself into Dabria's abdomen. Slowly rising to her feet, Veronica stood over Dabria's lifeless body.

"That's what you get, you crazy little bitch," shouted Veronica. She looked down at Dabria, spat on her and walked out the front door, collapsing on the front lawn. Moments later, Doctor Whittman pulled up in her car.

"Veronica, are you OK? Where's Dabria?"

"No, I'm not. It seems like my arm is broken. Who's Dabria?"

"My guess is that you didn't receive any of my messages," exclaimed Doctor Whittman. Well for now, let's call her Shantell and after we get you some help, I'll explain everything on the way to the hospital. Where's Tom?"

"Dead, Tom's dead," Veronica said, sadly.

"And Shantell, where is she?"

"She's dead too. I killed her, but only after she tried to kill me, I didn't want to do it. While I was defending myself, she lost control. It's like it wasn't even her," said Veronica.

"In a way, she wasn't. Let's get you to the hospital. Detective Chase and the police are already coming. He's the one that figured it all out. In the hospital trauma ward, Veronica laid, receiving treatment for a broken arm and several fractured ribs, while Doctor Whittman sat next to her, divulging all the information she was aware of.

However, Detective Chase and Segura conveniently omitted the peculiar details involving voodoo rituals, soul trading, and the non-existent adoption agency that they used to adopt Shantell. The account would only serve to further fuel speculation and uncertainty. Following their conversation with Veronica and providing further details about their perspective, Detective Chase and Segura strolled over to the neighboring building. They positioned themselves by a small window, observing a room filled with two police officers.

"Do you think she'll ever wake up Segura?"

"I'm uncertain about many things now, including whether she'll wake up Chase. I'm surprised she's still alive."

Detective Chase shook his head in disbelief and

quietly asked Segura if the plan to harm her was still in play. Witnessing her defenseless condition, lying unconscious with a mechanical ventilator, it made him reconsider his intention to kill her.

"Although I'm unsure, I have a responsibility to do it in case she recovers. I won't make the same mistake I made 11 years ago. I will stick around just in case she wakes up to finish the job. The only thing left was an internal struggle within Dabria's thoughts, as she found Shantell patiently waiting for her, yet unable to summon the energy to take back control and retaliate. "I thought I got rid of you," said Dabria.

"No, I've been here watching everything, and I'll keep you here. Even if I'm unconscious until they unplug me. So, Dabria, just sit back, because I'm here to stay.